ALSO BY TREVOR TUCKER

Ned Kelly's Son

A saga of Australian heritage ... almost lost in history.

The Stolen Maps

Australia's greatest maritime secret?

Aussie Anecdotes

A collection of quintessential Australian short stories.

A Sense of Justice

A tale of retribution for two unlikely Australian heroes.

God only knows when.

A look at the criminal underbelly of rural Australia and the consequences
of farm invasion and stock theft.

WONNANGATTA

TREVOR TUCKER

TREVOR TUCKER PUBLISHING

A catalogue record for this
book is available from the
National Library of Australia

FOREWORD

Two murders occurred between late 1917 and 1918 at the remote Wonnangatta Valley in East Gippsland, Victoria, Australia. The victims were Jim Barclay, the manager of Wonnangatta Station, and John Bamford, a cook and general hand.

Theories have since abounded regarding the perpetrators; some controversial, some nonsense, and a few, quite close to the mark.

Historically, verdicts of murder, by a person or persons unknown were formally handed down in both instances.

These weren't the only murders which occurred in this same period—all in similar surroundings—but those deaths never made it into the public domain.

Regardless, the Barclay and Bamford cases have never been officially solved ... unless the validity of this account is accepted as more than circumstantial.

1

I knew the "little earner" I'd created couldn't last forever. Little, be buggered, it was a substantial operation.

With nobody to answer to but myself, nevertheless my chosen trade was a tad risky. Incredibly, because there was no practical opposition from local graziers, and currently no organised police interference, I was raking in the cash.

My trade, though frowned upon by many, was an essential service to the timber workers harvesting cedar in the remote Dorrigo region of New South Wales. In fact, their lives depended upon me. So, you see, I was active in the exploitation business, transferring meat to those hardworking axemen. Not my meat of course, that all belonged to unsuspecting, careless, and lazy graziers.

Yes, my monopoly operation was fundamentally illegal, but no one was being physically harmed, and on balance, the local blacks were willing and peaceful benefactors so long as I paid them on time and kept the grog up to them.

But, unbeknown to me, things were about to change!

Competition had also emerged, but worse, men were now hunting me, to put a bullet in my head and collect a sizeable bounty.

And, behind the closed doors of political party meeting rooms in

Canberra, cattle duffing had firmly captured the attention of Australia's sympathetic lawmakers.

Good God, please give me a break.

* * *

OF COURSE, such rhetoric is far too expansive to appear on the headstone of a felon's grave, regardless of how famous or infamous.

Nevertheless, the forgoing admission typified the lives of many who had lost their way.

2

———

I was born Leon Douglas Hart in 1881, Bristol, England, an only child in a disintegrating marriage.

Bristol was a rapidly developing and important trading town located on the river Avon, a place of real opportunity for most who lived there; but not so for my parents who lost their well-paid jobs, both fired for being argumentative troublemakers.

Unfortunately, my parents had simultaneously fallen victim to the merciless grip of the demon grog and refused to acknowledge their reliance upon it; often unaware they had left me alone to fend for myself, not caring if I was hungry, cold, and frightened.

As an infant, I don't recall any enjoyable family times but do recall events which upset me with increasing regularity. For instance, at my fourth birthday party. Those who attended, soon departed (most of them crying) to their homes when my drunken mother disrespectfully reprimanded those who hadn't given me a birthday present. 'Bloody useless lot of so-called friends; go on, shove off the lot of yah,' she yelled at them. I seldom met those kids again.

The worst event occurred on the second day I attended school. No one was there to collect me at day's end. Somehow, I safely found my way home, albeit now a house stripped of all its goods and chattels; no sign of my parents, and not even a "sorry son" note.

The dreadful reality of being abandoned suddenly consumed me: a child should never expect to be betrayed this way. Totally confused and terrified I slumped onto the front steps and bawled.

I never did see my parents again and never saw any need to search for them.

* * *

OLD MAN RONNIE ROSSER, who lived in the house opposite, rescued me. He had seen what had unfolded during that day and admitted to me (about three years later) that he was glad to see the last of my parents. But he too had not expected they would be so heartless to just dump me with nothing but the clothes I was wearing.

What I thought would be a neighbourly overnight stay, turned into many wonderful years under Ron's, and then his son's care. We all got on famously. I now miraculously had the grand-father I always wanted with Ronnie, and a father, Max, to look up to. So, it seemed only right my adopted name became, Leon Rosser.

Regrettably, Ron's health was deteriorating quickly. He was admitted to an old age infirmary in Bristol, but not before he arranged for me to live with Max and his wife, Elspeth, who owned a farm in rural Gloucestershire. Their ongoing support and guidance never diminished, and I got on well with my three stepsiblings, Fay (the eldest), Bertie (next youngest) and Paul (the youngest). Decent folk, all of them, so I guess I was entitled to later become the black sheep.

Nevertheless, as expected of me in this near perfect guardianship arrangement, I worked hard around the farm, got good school results, tried to be punctual, and saved whatever money came my way. I enjoyed every task and I'm proud I excelled in all four.

It also surprised me how quickly I became adept at riding horses: I had a natural sense of camaraderie with all four of Max's horses who each willingly transported me to many out of the way places of neighbouring counties. This animal attraction was not confined to horses; sheep and cattle handling came easily to me and would play a major part in my later life.

As a matter of fact, it was during this time of exploration I also took a wrong turn, not in terms of forgetting the way home, but rather, I had a compelling belief that Max would be delighted if his flock of sheep was supplemented by a few more head relieved from unwitting neighbours. I never confessed those thefts, nor did Max suspect my involvement: if he did, he never raised it with me.

When I turned fifteen, I dreamt of one day having my own farm, confident in my fifth, and most effective latent ability: an unexpected liking for planning ahead and converting opportunity to my favour.

For example, I often quizzed Max on everything he knew about Australia and repeatedly dangled the potential of unimaginable prosperity and health benefits in that distant country ... for all our family. Eventually, Max and Elspeth eagerly announced a major decision *they(?)* had been pondering for months. The prospect of free, abundant, fertile farming land, and accommodation upon arrival, was far too enticing an opportunity to consider forever remaining in England. Fortuitously, they felt it fitting I should accompany them.

So, I too, became a free settler in that new country much sooner than I had anticipated. As exciting a prospect this immigration proved, the sailing was tediously rough, uncomfortable, and often terrifying. On several occasions I recall feeling utterly dreadful, unceremoniously heaving overboard in company with one or more of my equally stricken family members, contemplating death by drowning as surely the preferred way to die.

Disembarking at Melbourne, I vowed to myself that *nothing* would ever get me to return by ship to England.

* * *

Upon arrival at Customs, my stepsiblings and I were soon in for a very well-concealed surprise.

In just a few seconds, most unexpectedly, Max was joyfully

embracing an old, scruffily dressed and heavily bearded man. Obviously, somehow, they knew each other. After much backslapping, smiles and vigorous handshakes, Max said enthusiastically, 'I'd like you all to meet Uncle Vincent. He's going to take us to our destination.

'It wasn't easy, but Elspeth and I deliberately kept this surprise from you children. And, I'll have you know, it was Vincent's older brother, Ron, who first floated this idea years ago.'

'Yeah, well maybe he did,' I reflected, *'but it was my influence which finally pushed Max and Elspeth into making "their good sense decision" to leave England.'*

'Anyway, Max continued, 'Vincent has kept his word to meet us, and I'm sure he'll keep an eye on us.'

'Hang on there just a bit, Max,' Vincent replied in a clear, confident fashion. 'I go by the name "Rocky" around here, so please let's not confuse the locals, eh?

'Anyway, welcome all. But before we have a good chat, let's grab your luggage and get me wagon loaded.'

An hour and a half later, with help from two of Rocky's strong wharfie mates eager to make a bob or two, the wagon was fully loaded with our only worldly belongings which were then secured in place with stout ropes and amazing non-slip knots.

Having thanked and paid our hired help, Rocky ushered us into a tea house opposite the dock, a slightly elevated location from where we could keep watch on our wagon and the horses.

Rocky had brought five horses with him, one to pull the wagon and four others—complete with saddles and bridles—for us kids to ride. I was last to enter the teahouse, having lingered behind to acquaint myself with these beasts, all of which seemed at ease to allow me to run my hands over their muzzles and gently tug their ears.

'You're a bloody lucky young fella!' Rocky confronted me as I walked into the tea house. 'Last time a bloke tried to pat me horses, he lost two fingers: bit clean off his right hand. You're gunna have tah tell me where you learnt that sort of stuff.'

* * *

A VERY PLEASANT meal and half an hour later, we were on our way. Rocky, Elspeth and Max were sitting shoulder to shoulder on the wagon driver's bench, leading, and us kids following, me at the rear in case any of my stepsiblings got into difficulties with their assigned mount.

Every few miles, I pushed my horse forward to walk beside those up front. As I came abreast of each animal I would lean from my saddle and either stroke its face or firmly pat and rub its neck while simultaneously muttering my endearments and encouragement. None of them objected, but rather, seemed glad of my attentions.

Each time we stopped for a meal break or to find a suitable toilet spot, I lavished attention on my horse, then upon the wagon horse, seeing to it they had no stones lodged under their shoes, nor leg joint "hot spots". More than once, I looked up and noticed Rocky watching me as I went about my tasks. I'd smile and he would return that smile while slowly shaking his head, as if in disbelief, I'm sure.

I must have shamed Fay, Bertie, and Paul by my actions, because Max soon gave them an earful. 'Come on you three, you can't leave all the work to Leon. Get your lazy backsides moving and do your bit to help.'

'Yeah, come on,' I said jovially enough, 'you just might enjoy it ... and besides, yah might learn something.'

Each day, Rocky would seek out my company away from the others. For about half an hour or so, we'd happily talk about horses, some of the places he'd lived and worked in his youth and, it seemed to me, that I was being tested ... as if he had something in mind for me, but never really got around to telling me exactly what that might be.

On the other hand, Rocky was never rude nor disrespectful to the others; always polite and he easily cultivated an open, rapport. Most evenings as the tree's shadows advanced across the plains, and that amazing interval when the flies had retreated and before the mosquitoes came lusting after our blood, our dinner would be eaten in quiet, relaxed camaraderie.

3

____

We headed north towards the town of Wangaratta, then east towards a distant mountain range. 'The Great Dividing Range,' Rocky nonchalantly advised us while nodding in their general direction, 'but we've only got twelve miles to go before arriving at the property. It's a deceptive view, but those mountains are another twenty-five miles or so further east.'

Mind you, it had taken us fifteen days of slog to get this far: so, no need just then, to break our normal routine and charge off.

There had been no home comforts afforded us during that travelling time, other than those provided by the few overnight guest house stopovers recommended by Rocky. The country through which we travelled was varied, vast and beautiful, but the passing of each day left us bored and lethargic, even though most of the time we were all sitting. Regardless, Rocky would call a halt every two hours, whereupon we'd gladly walk beside our mounts to not only give them a breather, but also for us, an opportunity to massage our aching backsides and leg muscles.

The early November weather was very kind to us; generally bright and sunny. The only clouds, high above, were swept into white, feathery skeins reaching from horizon to horizon.

The roads and tracks which Rocky expertly navigated, were generally in reasonable condition allowing us to make good progress. Passing traffic was minimal and usually in good humour.

Elspeth and Fay had had the foresight to bring their umbrellas, but initially, us men only had wide-brimmed hats to keep the worst of the sun from unprotected limbs and exposed ear tips. Thanks to Rocky's nous, we novice English folk soon learnt the benefit of wearing button-down long-sleeved shirts and to raise one's shirt collar to get some additional relief from the sun.

Fortunately, there were few occasions throughout each day when a cooling breeze wasn't blowing to take some of the edge off the temperature.

Our wagon horse had shown great stamina and had immediately settled into his task from day one and shown a responsiveness and work ethic that I'd never witnessed previously. 'A "waler"', Rocky was quick to proudly point out, 'by far me best and most important animals I've got; you'll see.'

Apart from the first day when our allotted mounts misbehaved, they too had settled into a daily rhythm without too much protest thereafter.

* * *

It was not unexpected that nobody greeted us when we finally arrived at the property. But that was easily overlooked as I cast my eyes upon the magnificent sights surrounding this place.

The landscape was flat to undulating, and giant red gum eucalyptus trees were scattered throughout the near and medium distance. To the east was the telltale sign of a river judging by the continuous band of growth of different trees as far as the eye could see in both directions: the Ovens River. And of course, to the north and further east, loomed Mount Buffalo.

Post and rail fencing skirted and divided Rocky's property into several well grassed paddocks; clearly, establishing his boundaries would have been a massive task. Three windmills were strategically positioned to catch any breeze, ensuring a constant supply of water for any stock; but right then, a little strange I thought, there was no stock to be seen.

To our left was a neat, but small and most rustically constructed cottage, and an adjacent, decrepit long drop toilet which obviously also had functionality in mind ahead of an inviting design. An equally decrepit lean-to at the rear of the hut completed the domestic layout. However, about a hundred yards to the north was another building, almost hidden by a stand of eucalypt trees which I would later learn was a purpose-built slaughterhouse.

I rode up to the wagon just as it came to a halt at the property's entrance gate. 'Well, this is it folks,' said Rocky cheerfully. 'Here, Leon, you'll need this'. I leaned from my saddle and accepted the offered key.

I dismounted, opened the gate's rather large padlock then easily hauled the well-hinged gate wide open.

As I led my horse through the gate, I looked up to see Max's face; obviously shocked, mouth wide open, staring in disbelief in the direction of the cottage. In that instant, a very agitated Elspeth stood up from the wagon's bench seat, put her hands on her hips, turned to confront Rocky and then proceeded to shout at him on top note.

'You rotten bloody scoundrel, Rocky!' she let fly. 'You've dragged us halfway around the world … to this! Why in God's name would you do this to us? You've not only deceived us, but you've betrayed us to boot! Good God man, even a blind man would know seven people can't live in that hovel; what are you playing at? I'm going to report you to the police at the first opportunity and, and … '

I'd never witnessed anything like this from Elspeth; her usual calm and softly spoken demeanour had disappeared, totally.

By this stage, Max was also on his feet. And, judging by the ferocious look of menace on his face and his bunched fists, for a moment I thought he was about to knock Rocky's head off.

'Sit down; both of you, and listen,' Rocky interrupted, albeit while trying to stifle a laugh. 'I'm sure you both wanted a surprise, but this ain't it.'

Max and Elspeth glanced at each other, then gradually sat down. Like me, they were baffled, and understandably both relieved.

'Leon, please close the gate after we pass through; there's a good lad,' Rocky asked casually, 'and snib the padlock. Hang onto that key but keep it safe, and don't lose it!'

Rocky flicked the reins, and the wagon horse moved forward along a well-defined, two-wheel track which by-passed the cottage and headed towards the northern horizon of the paddock.

'Now, Max, if you would,' Rocky asked quietly, 'call the kids and have 'em ride ahead with Leon to the top of this rise. And tell 'em to stop there and wait for us to catch up.'

4

———

As Rocky brought the wagon to a halt at the crest of the hill, I turned in my saddle just in time to see Elspeth's demeanour change from tight-lipped disinterest and coldness, to disbelief, then astonishment. Initially her eyes and mouth flew wide open, but her right hand quickly covered her mouth. Her posture also altered abruptly; her head jerking upright in unison with her suddenly ramrod straight back; her shoulders squared. With her left hand she brushed off her hat, and slowly started to stand, not that by doing so the view before her could have been improved ... and I'm sure I heard her say, 'Good God almighty, Rocky; you really are a sneaky bastard!'

Max's reaction was different: the headlock he had put on Rocky was possibly a bit too strong, but they were both laughing good naturedly. 'Now that's what I call a surprise, you cunning old devil; but I love you to bits,' Max said as he released Rocky, then punched him on the shoulder as if to reinforce his words.

Before us was an almost breathtaking sight: in a clearing near the bottom of a densely populated valley of native trees, sat the most splendid homestead of traditional colonial design. Green corrugated iron sheeting adorned the roof and a wrap-around veranda, while the exterior was white and accommodated many glazed windows. The veranda was raised requiring a few steps; however, there were no handrails.

A robust chimney stood proudly to one side dominating the roof. I later learnt that this huge chimney was made from rocks selected from the creek which ran past the house about fifty yards away.

A smaller building whose architecture mimicked the house stood closely nearby, a pantry or wash house perhaps.

About forty yards from the house, a large shed sat nestled between a post and rail fence, and close behind were stock holding yards.

Realising what had just unfolded, I swung my horse around and charged down the valley with Fay, Bertie, and Paul in close pursuit.

Arriving at the house, we dismounted and quickly hitched our horse's reins to the hitching rail. Breaking our necks to inspect inside the house we all charged for the front door.

However, we were suddenly confronted by a black man who most unexpectedly appeared from a side veranda holding a shotgun, albeit brandishing it with just the right amount of menace to put a halt to our impatient charge.

'Hang on you lot,' he said firmly as he pressed himself between us and the house's fly-wire front door. 'Where's your manners? Just wait here until the owner arrives, he might not want to let you into his home!'

I was about to argue the toss with this somewhat belligerent fellow, but he was saved by the arrival of Rocky's wagon. Max almost threw himself to the ground and then rushed around the wagon, presumably to help Elspeth alight. But Max needn't have done so for she was already walking toward the veranda steps, unashamedly looking to-and-fro, smiling like a loon, and muttering, 'Oh my God, Max, isn't this just so beautiful. C'mon, let's see inside, eh?'

Had Rocky not intervened, Elspeth would have walked straight into the black fellow. 'Thanks, Adam,' Rocky quickly called out, 'would you take care of the horses please, then join us for a cuppa.'

Only then did Elspeth register the presence of Adam; quickly stepping back in shock and bewilderment and nearly losing her balance ... only to be saved by Adam who grabbed her by the wrist to prevent her from falling from the veranda.

Adam then resumed his position, determined it seemed, to prevent any of us from entering the house. 'Boots off first,' he stipulated, albeit smiling broadly as he stood aside and held the front door open.

As Elspeth walked past Adam, it didn't go unnoticed that she reached out and touched his arm and said quietly, 'thank you, Adam.'

* * *

I WAS ABOUT to take my boots off but hung back. The folly of my earlier confidence—that I should have "dealt with Adam"—had sensibly evaporated. He was not only over six feet tall, but well-built, athletic ... very black, and obviously much stronger than me.

His face intrigued me: receding short curly hair, prominent eyebrows, deep brown eyes, clean shaven face, and perfect, white teeth.

But it was his disposition which intrigued me most; a natural friendliness, and a ready smile, nevertheless assertive without being overbearing.

A hundred questions competed for attention in my brain, but the best I could come up with, was, 'I say, Adam, are there any fish to be had in that creek?'

'Oh yes, if you know where to look,' Adam replied, 'mainly trout and blackfish in the larger pools. You can test your luck later this arvo if you'd like.'

'That'd be great, but we don't have any rods or reels,' I replied, somewhat dejected, 'and, besides, what would I use for bait?'

'Don't worry about rods, we've got several, though they're not necessary to catch trout; I'll teach you how to tickle 'em. On the other hand, we'll need rods for the blackfish: you can only catch them late in the afternoon as the sun's going down, and early into the night.

'As for bait, well Leon, how about you go and get settled into your new house, while I turn the horses out. I'll be back shortly to help unload the wagon. Easiest if you all offload as much as possible and spread it along the veranda. That way you can more quickly identify your personal belongings and get it inside before we tackle the heavier stuff.

'After I've put the wagon away, I'll meet you here, around five thirty. Then we'll collect some bait and head off upstream to some good fishing spots I know. Oh yes, bring an old sock with you, one without any holes.

With that organised, Adam said as he walked away, 'see you then, but don't tell your brothers and sister; we don't want them tagging along, not yet anyway.

'And don't forget to let Rocky know you're going fishing with me, OK?'

Tickling trout, collecting bait, and learning how to handle a rod and reel, plus the prospect of night fishing for blackfish was, well, exciting ... but the need for a sock had me puzzled.

As I removed my boots, I could hear Fay, Bertie, and Paul inside, laughing and talking excitedly, each claiming their room to be the best. Max met me in the hallway and directed me to my own room, yes, my own room; my own bed, my own floor to ceiling windows which doubled as a door allowing me to access the side veranda, blackout curtains, my own wardrobe, my own bookshelf, floor rugs, a lockable door ... and best of all, the unexpected luxury of privacy.

I then found Rocky in the kitchen with a very attentive Elspeth, showing her the ropes on how to best control the stove's fire without either burning any meals, or herself, and how to keep the fire just hot enough to keep the kettle boiling all day for that ever-necessary cup of tea.

As Rocky stood up after feeding the fire one last piece of wood, and before he could move on to explain anything else, I walked up to him, offered my hand, and said, 'I dunno what I've done to deserve this Rocky, but thank you so much.'

'A pleasure son,' Rocky replied, 'now go and see if your father needs a hand, eh?'

5

An hour later the wagon was finally empty. Adam then led the horse with the wagon attached into the large storage shed which allowed the wagon to enter at one end, and to be driven from the other end without restriction. A clever arrangement which meant all harnessing, loading, and unloading could be undertaken while protected from either the sun, or rain, or wind.

After transferring and positioning my few belongings into my room, I wandered outside again to more closely inspect this truly magnificent house and its surrounds. All exterior walls of the house and its outbuildings were painted white, hiding milled red gum, tongue-in-groove wallboards.

The veranda was also made from milled red gum, albeit much thicker, then oiled for long term preservation.

Looking up the valley, Mount Buffalo loomed huge in the distance. Close by, I could hear the small creek babbling along as it made its way to the Ovens River. And there was no lack of bird life competing for my attention: tiny wrens, some with bright blue tail feathers flittered between nearby shrubs, white-winged choughs paraded about in happy families and kookaburras occasionally burst into laughter.

* * *

TRUE TO HIS WORD, Adam arrived on time carrying two rods and a small shoulder bag. 'You've got the sock that I suggested?' he asked as he handed one of the rods to me.'

'Yes, but what's it for?'

'Well, one of the best baits for trout are live grasshoppers. You've already seen many different types of 'em jumping around, and some with yellow wings which make that "clacking" noise as they fly away when you disturb them. During the hottest time of the day, they're all at their most active, and very hard to catch. However, they all slow down as the evening approaches, particularly if a cool change arrives, makin' 'em much easier to catch.

'But, since we're going to need twenty or so, how do you reckon you're going to keep 'em secure and still leave both your hands free to use your rod and reel?'

I got it, and burst out, 'The sock!'

'Right, so now, give it to me and let me show you how to secure 'em.'

With that said, Adam moved quickly and soon caught two good sized hoppers. 'Here, watch this.' Gradually he rolled back the neck of the sock then thrust both insects to the toe end. Surprisingly, neither hopper was able to use its strong back legs to kick free, the spines on their legs having firmly snagged on the loose fibres of the sock. He then rolled the sock back into its normal shape, twisted the neck a few turns, then thrust the bunched up, twisted end firmly behind my belt.

'Right, now show me how you'd retrieve 'em before putting 'em onto your hook.'

I fumbled getting the sock from my belt, but then carefully rolled it open until a hopper came into view. I plucked it free of the restraining fibres and then, instinctively, quickly started to roll back the neck of the sock to prevent its partner making a break for unplanned freedom.

Of course, I was too slow; I dropped the first hopper. The second one suddenly kicked and was airborne in a flash of whirring bright yellow wings, and a clicking sound as if telling me, 'You'll have ta do better than that to catch me chum.'

Understandably Adam saw the humour in that lesson but held his laughter in check. 'You'll soon get the hang of things Leon, yah just need a bit more practise.'

Once we'd caught about thirty hoppers and consigned them to my sock, Adam called a halt. For the next fifteen minutes or so, he first demonstrated how to rig the line; no sinker, just a single hook attached using a very easy, universal, non-slip knot. He next demonstrated how to feed the hopper onto the hook, and how to cast the lightly weighted line; always upstream he emphasised, for trout can only survive by facing into flowing water, which must pass over their gills.

'I think you're ready Leon,' Adam said confidently, 'so let's now catch a fish or two. I'll go first; you watch me carefully how I make the cast, and to where I put the bait. Don't rush things; the rocks are slippery, and you don't want a wet backside.'

I watched in awe as Adam slowly waded into the creek, no more than three steps. He stopped, balanced himself, then gracefully lobbed his hopper about fifteen feet upstream to a run of crystal-clear water close to the opposite bank. Relentlessly, the current dragged the hopper deeper into the pool which beckoned beneath a section of scrub whose branches overhung the creek's bank.

As soon as I lost sight of the hopper, the loose line trailing the bait zipped forward, upstream, vigorously pulling down the tip of Adam's rod. Adam didn't strike immediately but waited about three seconds; only then striking, downstream, to set the hook. Those few seconds were to become the difference between assured success and a disappointing loss; the interval being the time necessary for the fish to turn and face upstream, and to commence feeding. Without that hesitation, the bait would invariably be yanked from the fish's mouth.

Adam easily landed the fish which he estimated to be a one-pound rainbow trout, then, after wetting his hands removed the hook. 'If the fish you catch ever swallows the hook completely, and you don't want to keep your catch, don't try to remove the hook,' he said compassionately, 'or you'll probably kill it; so just cut the line and release it.'

That said, he returned the fish to the creek, walked up the bank, then removed his shoulder bag and handed it to me.

'Here, you keep this, it's got all you need in it in case you get broken off or snagged … and it's somewhere to put your keepers.

'OK Leon, it's your turn. I'm heading back to the house, so you've got the creek to yourself. Keep an eye on the time and be back at the house before dark. Good luck; see you then.' That said, he strode off.

Though excited, I was thankful for Adam's departure, not that I didn't enjoy his company, I really did, but more so that I didn't want anyone watching as I made my maiden attempts to catch something; anything.

I admit to underestimating the difficulty of bait casting; however, I was soon presenting my hapless grasshoppers at least as far as Adam had done. The more difficult task was not slipping on the rocks and going arse-over-head into very cold water.

So absorbed was I in my new challenge I had no idea that Adam had not immediately returned to the house but instead made a detour upstream and hid where he could observe my progress. This I only discovered later in the evening after my return to the house to display my catch, four beautiful rainbows, at least two of which were larger than Adam had caught.

Adam volunteered to show me how to scale and gut my catch and when we were out of ear shot, he admitted to his subterfuge. 'You're a quick learner Leon,' he said enthusiastically, as he made sure I got to clean three of my catch, 'but that big one you lost on the second pool was just a bit too smart, eh? You waited too long before striking; had you snagged before you realised that he had your hopper. A good lesson learnt, I'd say.' He was right of course.

With Rocky supervising, Elspeth cooked my catch with great care. There was plenty for all of us to enjoy only because Bertie and Paul turned up their noses and refused to even try the smallest morsal of those succulent trout.

6

———————

That night the others all retired early, leaving Rocky, myself and Adam sitting in comfortable high-backed woven cane chairs positioned strategically on the side veranda, drinking hot, sweetened, black tea. It had been a big day, but the cool night air seemed to sharpen my senses. Though now nearly seventeen, I felt honoured to be included in the company of two, much older and likeable blokes.

The conversation was amiable but soon turned to horses and how Rocky put them to use.

'Well son, they're all what we call walers,' he started to explain.

'As you can see, they're all about fifteen and a half, to sixteen hands and all have the same brown colour; but they've each got their own personality. They're great workers with incredible stamina, always alert, particularly when it comes to cattle work.'

'What he means is,' Adam was quick to clarify, 'particularly when it comes to mustering and moving them back and forwards between here and the Dargo High Plains; depends on where the best feed is to be had. Normally, in early summer, we push several mobs up onto the high country, where it's cooler and the feed and water is abundant. They fatten up quickly, but as winter approaches we have a general muster: most of 'em remain on the lower slopes within the Buckland Valley, but the ones we want to sell get pushed back here.'

'I've noticed you ride well, Leon,' Rocky added enthusiastically, 'but have you ever ridden in mountain country?'

'There're no mountains where I come from in England,' I replied. 'Pretty, yes, but just flat or undulating country mostly. Why do you ask Rocky?'

'It so happens that I need to bring thirty or so head down from the high country, or "the Top" as we usually call it; while they're still in their best possible condition,' Rocky replied, then seriously added, 'and the sooner rather than later, while I can demand the best prices for them.'

'I'd love to help out,' I added enthusiastically, unwittingly having taken the bait which both Adam and Rocky had cast in my direction. 'I'm pretty good with horses. And yeah, I reckon I can manage a bit of mountain work. So, when are you planning to do this?'

'Not until Max and Elspeth give you permission,' Rocky replied intently, 'and not until you can convince us you are not wanted by the police.'

That last remark was most unexpected.

'Look, I turn eighteen soon' I added, just a bit put out that anyone might suspect I could not be trusted. 'Max and Elspeth will probably welcome me being out from under their feet and supervision. And I give you my word that I've never done anything which attracted the attention of police. However, on a few occasions I did relieve some wealthy neighbours of a few sheep.'

That said, Rocky and Adam quickly looked at each other; eyes wide open and eyebrows raised, followed by what I correctly interpreted were nods of approval.

'By the way,' I probed, 'do we go onto Mount Buffalo?'

'No, not on this muster,' Rocky replied, 'but you'll go to the head of the Buckland Valley where you'll then turn east and follow a few secret tracks before arriving at the Dargo High Plains. You'll see some beautiful country; I can guarantee that.

'Anyway, it'll be just Adam and you, young man, so do as you're told, or he'll kick your arse! Given that you're likely to be away for about eight days, I hope you're OK with that arrangement Leon?'

'Yeah, but why aren't you coming with us, Rocky?'

'None of your business at the moment,' Rocky replied with just a bit of venom, 'but suffice to say I've got arrangements to make with potential buyers. You just make sure none of my cattle get lost on the way home. Now, go and have a chat with Max and Elspeth; but out of earshot of your brothers and sister, OK?'

'And don't worry about not going up onto Mount Buffalo,' Adam chimed in. 'It ain't going nowhere. I'll take them up there after we return; after your backside has recovered.'

* * *

MAX AND ELSPETH gave me their unconditional approval, though had they not, I would have taken off, regardless. Bertie and Paul could not have cared less when I outlined my upcoming adventure for them: we had never been close and seldom in the past had we shared lengthy periods of time together and, true to form, they both showed no real interest in my upcoming excursion on this occasion.

I sometimes worried about these two lads: one petulant and scheming, the other easily led and riddled with a disturbing "be cruel to animals' obsession".

Fay, on the other hand, wanted to tag along. Rocky compromised, saying, 'Now listen here, young lady. I don't underestimate your riding ability, but where your brother's headed is not the place for you just now. But I tell you what. You can ride with us for a few hours or so, then you'll need to return here; OK?'

This was accepted by Fay, though I'm pretty sure she was more than just a bit miffed. She turned to Adam and said, 'well then, can I come with you when you two go onto Mount Buffalo?'

'We'll see,' Adam replied, 'but it'll depend on the climate somewhat.'

I'm not sure, exactly, what made me uneasy; maybe it was the way

Adam hesitated over the word "climate" or, perhaps, it was a veiled implication of something entirely different.

Only the arrival of unseasonal snow and cold winds could make Adam's offer impossible to fulfill, but summer was months from turning to Autumn.

Little did I know then that I was still being sized up to test my loyalties; to keep my mouth shut about our intended high plains muster, and to see if I had worked out that this muster might have unexpected consequences.

However, it suddenly hit me: what I was about to partake in was probably not legal, that the police might soon be looking for us, and that Mount Buffalo probably offered Rocky and Adam—and *me*—asylum from the law. And to be frank, this realisation sent a shiver of excitement down my back.

My decision was easy; I'd keep my mouth shut for there would be plenty of time later to privately quiz Rocky about how he came upon his obvious wealth. What surprised me most though, was how quickly I was prepared to sacrifice a secure family life to embrace one of crime.

7

Two days later, we set off with a few final words of encouragement from Max and Elspeth, some waving of hands ... and with Fay tagging along, chirping with excitement.

However, beforehand, but not unexpectedly, Rocky had led Adam out of earshot just before we departed, no doubt with final instructions which would be known only to them. They too seemed somewhat excited, not arguing the toss, but more like agreeing on directions and suitable stopover points. I noticed they then shook hands, as good friends would do.

Adam and I each had two horses, one to ride, one as a pack horse. I chose the same horse which I had ridden from Melbourne; his name was *Guppy*. The packhorse I chose was *Joey*, also a waler with whom I had quickly bonded.

Fay followed my example of choice of mount, but Adam's selections were his favourites, both also walers, and both experienced from several previous high-country musters.

I had never slept on the ground in a canvas swag, nor packed saddle bags. So, it was a great lesson received from both Rocky and

Adam who patiently showed me how to do that most economically to include my pillow, blankets and (essential only) clothes, then how to roll up the swag, tighten its binding straps and finally how to secure it across Joey's back.

One half of the saddle bags were packed with a bag of flour for damper, small packets of powdered milk and sultanas, containers of salt, and pepper, two boxes of tea, a bag of sugar, a small box of matches, a single steak knife, spoon and a fork, a steel pannikin, and a tea-towel.

The other half of the saddle bag was packed with a change of clothes, several pairs of socks, two towels, newspaper cut into meaningfully sized squares for toilet paper, a small bag of Rocky's home-made barley sugar, hobbles for my horses ... and a small cloth bag containing something which Adam said was a surprise from Rocky, 'for later on.'

Adam demonstrated how to secure the saddle bag to Guppy, then removed it, and had me repeat the job. That task was relatively simple, but the real trick was going to be remembering on which side everything had been packed.

Just before mounting up, Rocky had demonstrated how to attach Joey's leading rope to the rear of my saddle. 'Mind you, son, you'll probably not need this for long, he'll just follow, you'll see: Adam will let yah know when to remove it.'

* * *

About an hour later we crossed the Ovens River bridge at Porepunkah. We then reined in, and Adam wasted no time in farewelling Fay. Her face fleetingly showed disappointment, but that soon passed as she wheeled her horse around, smiled alluringly at me, then said, 'Thanks Adam, be safe and look after Leon for me.'

After she had crossed back over the bridge, Fay, smiling broadly, turned in her saddle and blew me a kiss with a hand gesture. I don't think Adam saw it, for he seemed intent upon getting a move on. At that distance my "little stepsister" was no longer that: somehow, she appeared, well, different.

I dutifully returned her wave, even raised my wide brimmed hat in acknowledgement, but nevertheless I felt strangely unnerved I had not previously noticed her beautiful transformation.

8

———

About ten miles upstream, along the Buckland Valley and at the foot of Mount Buffalo which now loomed directly above us, Adam called a halt. He dismounted, removed a blackened billycan hanging from a clip attached to his swag, then walked toward the near bank of the river. 'I'll get some water,' he called to me over his shoulder. 'We'll need a fire, Leon. See if you can get one on the go to boil the billy.

'You can leave the horses; they know not to stray too far. And get your own mug if you want a cuppa.'

On his return, he went via his packhorse and removed a few items from his saddle bag. My fire was already a brilliant success and crackled nicely as if calling me to feed it more wood. Adam then placed the billy carefully on top of my fire. 'You can put a bit more wood around the billy,' Adam advised cheerfully, 'but don't let it tip over as the middle of your fire burns down.'

We didn't have to wait long for the billy to boil, at which time Adam threw into it, two handfuls of tea leaves. Using a stout tree branch about four feet long, he carefully retrieved the billy from the flames by its wire handle and then placed it on the ground.

After a few minutes he said, 'now watch this Leon,' whereupon he took hold of the billy's wire handle then started to "windmill" it, complete with its contents, about six times on one side of his body … without spilling a drop.

'Right, the tea's had time to draw and should be about the right temperature. If you want it sweetened, plonk a handful of sugar into your mug and I'll show you how to pour without any spills and not get burnt in the process.'

About fifteen minutes later, each of us having downed two mugs of piping hot tea while sitting in quiet companionship on a nearby log, Adam suddenly stood and again visited his saddlebag.

As he resumed his seat on the log, he nonchalantly handed me a small canvas bag. 'It's time for that surprise Rocky promised you. Go on; open it.'

The bag was unexpectedly weighty. As my hand closed around its contents, a cold shiver ran down my back as I slowly withdrew a handgun.

'That's a six-shooter Leon,' Adam said quietly, yet reassuringly. 'let's hope you don't have to use it. It's *definitely not a toy* and could be the difference between you staying alive or being stoney dead.'

'But I've never held a handgun in my life,' I began to protest.

'Well, I have,' Adam replied comfortingly, 'and I know how, and when to use it. You're a quick learner Leon, so let's get started. But first, I'll give you one, and only one piece of advice.'

'Which is?'

'Never, never, point that gun at me!

'But if anyone ever levels theirs at you, do whatever's necessary to look after yourself so you can live another day … which might mean shooting a bounty hunter, or even a copper.

'By the way, there's a box of ammo in your saddle bag: twenty-four bullets should be enough for a bit of target practise and to discourage any unexpected opposition to our activities.'

'Which means I not only have the means to shoot to kill, but I'm now a cattle thief.'

'Yep, that's about it,' Adam replied off-handedly. 'So, are you still with Rocky and me, or do you want out?'

'Oh, I'm in for the moment,' I replied cheekily, 'so long as I get well paid, eh.'

* * *

For the next hour, Adam not only patiently taught me how to load the six-shooter, but to safely remove a bullet "hung up" in the firing mechanism, how to clean and oil the gun if it were put into storage ... and, most importantly, how to aim and shoot.

'I have to admit,' Adam announced at the end of some brief target practise. 'You're actually a bloody good shot, Leon. Just remember my initial advice regarding handling your gun. Here, take this holster and bullet belt; they're mine but keep them until you buy your own. Now load that belt and let's get a move on'.

Events may have been unfolding quickly, but I felt exhilarated to be recognised as a worthy adult and now seemingly empowered to be one.

It also occurred to me that my early teenage dream of owning my own farm was now potentially a reality. And damn it, the sudden image of Fay in my mind's eye, surprised me to such an extent causing an unfamiliar tingling in my gentleman's region.

Regardless, I made a pact with myself to insist that Adam drop his previous charade and to come clean about his history with Rocky, and how they expected me to contribute.

9

As the sun dipped below the horizon, I was surprised how quickly the temperature dropped. The going had been relatively easy so far, though the track's incline had increased, and we could only travel in single file. And, as Adam had said, the packhorses no longer needed to be led by rope; they just tagged along.

When a small clearing emerged between the surrounding timber, Adam called a halt. 'This'll do us nicely,' he said as he dismounted. 'We'll be out of any wind, that creek'll be handy, and there's a good pick for the horses.

'But first, let's relieve our horses of their saddles and bridles. Their hobbles can go on later, but they won't stray far in the meantime; you'll see.

'Now, follow me as I set up me swag. I probably snore, so you'll want to set up away from me; over there, I'd say, on that reasonably level patch next to the track. If there's any daylight left after we get set up, I'll see if I can tickle up a few trout for our dinner. And since you did such a good job earlier on getting a fire going, you may as well show me that wasn't a fluke.

'Over the years I've found many creeks just like this one; in fact, there's usually one in every valley. As you can see the water's crystal clear, it's cold and there's usually a trout or two wherever the undergrowth hangs over anything resembling a pool.

'Not that long ago,' Adam continued, 'these mountain creeks were swarming with gold prospectors from all over the world. Some became rich, but most departed emptyhanded. Apparently, the gold ran out, but there had been murderous "goings on" which left many Chinese dead and displaced before the law got things under control.'

'So, I gather there could still be some leftover gold in this creek?'

'Yep, but we haven't got time to put that to the test right now. Another time maybe; perhaps after we get our cattle back home.'

True to his word, after we had sorted our swags, I took my first lesson in how to prepare sultana damper. Only then did we head for the creek.

Adam removed his boots and socks, rolled up his trouser legs to above his knees and entered the creek. He slowly waded into a small pool, close to where the water exited. Painfully slowly, he leant forward and extended his arm beneath the water until it was up to his shoulder, and under the tussocky grass overhanging his position.

Maybe ten seconds passed. Then, in the blink of an eye, Adam wrenched his arm from the water, his fingers firmly holding a desperately flapping, slippery trout which was every bit of a foot long. Smiling, Adam heaved his catch up and over the bank, well clear of the creek. 'OK Leon, your go, see if you can beat that.'

All that I had to work on was Adam's earlier description of his tickling technique, but yes, I did beat his catch, not in size, but in quantity for I banked three more trout which became part of my first dinner under the stars.

It also seemed my fire making skills had not deserted me; that which I had built earlier was crackling along nicely for there was any amount of dry twigs and bark and larger branches lying about. Grilled trout, perfectly cooked sultana damper washed down with a mug of hot sweetened tea: a meal fit for Kings! And thieves.

A few early stars twinkled brightly against the night's intense blackness but were soon overwhelmed by the moon's glow as it rose above the mountain peaks.

We sat beside our fire within easy hearing distance of each other, but despite the warmth it radiated, we now wore our work jackets with their collars upturned to diminish a cold draft which seemed hell bent on brushing the back of our necks. Occasionally, one of us would feed more wood onto the fire causing a short-lived display of sparks and smoke to explode into the cold night air.

As the moon approached its zenith, the impact of its glow retreated as if welcoming every star in the universe to resume its place in one of nature's grandest displays, the magnificence of the Milky Way.

While stifling a yawn, my curiosity got the better of me. 'I say, Adam, can I ask you some questions about how you met Rocky?'

'Nah, not now. I'll fill you in tomorrow. I'm going to take a pee, then I'm turning in. I suggest you do too, but you'll need both of your blankets and your work jacket ... and wear your socks; I'm pretty sure there's going to be a frost.'

'But what about our horses' I asked. 'We can't leave 'em without putting their blankets on.'

'Somewhere in our saddle bags you'll find two horse blankets in each, and their hobbles. You're right, each night from here on, we'll need to do this, though they're tired and won't wander off.'

'OK. No hobbles. I'll take first turn to put their blankets on; I did that on many occasions on Max's farm back in England.'

'It's a deal, thanks Leon, and don't forget to turn the light out,' Adam chuckled.

My swag was more comfortable than I expected, and it wasn't long before I started drifting away to the accompaniment of the sounds of the night; nearby scurrying's of God knows what, the occasional squeak from small bats on the hunt for insects, dingoes howling up and down our valley trying to locate their mates ... and Adam's just bearable snoring.

* * *

ADAM WAS RIGHT; overnight a heavy frost had settled on our swags, and on everything else surrounding our camp site. There was a modest breeze, and the temperature must have been close to freezing, well below invigorating!

Regardless, I braved getting out of my swag whereupon my first realisation was to have a much-needed pee; but I also needed to get dressed bloody quickly and put on my boots before doing anything.

Dawn was on the way, but Adam was still snoring contentedly. The air smelt deliciously clean with just a hint of eucalyptus, so I inhaled deeply; too deeply because I suddenly had a coughing fit.

Although last night's fire was now just ashes, when I touched the ground beneath, it was still quite hot. Getting a new fire underway only took a few minutes, fuelled initially with a couple of sheets of newspaper (also known as toilet paper) and a handful of small dry twigs. Only a minute later I was successfully building up that infant fire with more, but much larger branches.

I didn't have to look far to locate our horses, all four greeted me with whinnies, gentle nudges, and their warm, steaming breaths. In single file they followed me back to the camp, then separated and started feeding on the nearby moisture laden grasses, and several different sedges. Adam stirred, though not yet fully awake, so I retrieved four chunks of barley sugar from my saddle bags and fed a piece to each horse.

Five minutes later when the billy was boiling, I added two handfuls of tea leaves and successfully "windmilled" the billy before letting the contents draw.

I next filled both of our pannikins with the steaming brew and threw a handful of sugar into each ... at which stage, Adam sat up from his swag, shivering. As he finished yawning, I handed him his pannikin. 'Good morning, sir,' I said cheekily, 'I trust you slept well and will now enjoy this sweet offering.

'Christ almighty, what time is it? And what's this?' Adam muttered in disbelief, I'm sure.

'We should have been underway by now, sir,' I said exaggerating a voice of practised servitude, 'but no-one will ever learn that you slept in. I'd suggest you get dressed before you freeze to death, sir, and not deprive yourself of the best mug of morning tea in the northeast.'

'Well, thankyee, mhar deehar boy,' Adam replied, playing along, 'most gracious of you to lavish such delights upon your master. Now, get your arse moving and bring in the horses.'

Smiling, I pointed in a most affectatious manner over his shoulder to where all four horses grazed serenely.

10

―――――

Later, during an extended morning tea break, Adam surprised me somewhat.

'Now Leon, two things. First, we're not far from our rendezvous where you'll meet some interesting men, some of whom are not the most savoury characters. So, from now on, wear your six-shooter and make sure you always have one up the spout … just in case like.

'And second, don't get *sucked in* by their foul language, or should they attempt to humiliate me. Ignore them as best you can. I'll sort them out if they attempt any rough neck stuff … and stick close to me, OK?'

'So why do you employ 'em, and put up with 'em?' I asked innocently.

'Because they get our job done at the right price, and because they keep their mouths shut.

'We'll press on in about an hour's time,' Adam continued, not showing any signs of building tension. 'Got any more questions in the meantime?'

I thought about this for half a minute then asked, 'Yes, many, but for starters, how is it you speak English, and how old are you?'

'Good questions; do you want the long or short versions?'

'The short version should suffice, but no bullshit, OK?' And whatever you tell me, will not be repeated ... fair enough?'

'I'm thirty-eight ... I think. The government of the day separated me and my two sisters from our parents, so that's a guess. I was about seven or eight years old then and I've never seen any of them since to confirm my true age ... which still upsets me now and then.

'I was placed in foster care but soon ran away. I was then secretly adopted by a sympathetic aboriginal family at a mission station on the Murray River, and that's when my luck changed.

'I was given an aboriginal name which I barely remember, but my stepfather liked the sound of, Adam. So, I became, Adam.

'When I was about fourteen, I was on my own, wandering the streets of Albury, bored, but feeling strangely convinced something good was about to happen. And it did ... almost immediately after that belief washed over me.

'I was sitting on the edge of the footpath watching a chap on the opposite side of the main street. He was carrying a huge load of items from the hardware store, back to his wagon, when he tripped and fell. I dashed across the street to see if he needed help, but soon learnt he'd broken his leg and was in considerable pain. The irony is that my unbelievably good fortune occurred at the expense of Rocky's bad luck. You've noticed he walks with a bit of a limp, eh?

'Anyway, no one else was about to lend a hand, so I somehow manoeuvred Rocky into the back of his wagon, along with all his recent purchases.'

'So, then what happened?' I asked with genuine interest.

'Rocky directed me to the hospital where they set his leg in plaster. I wasn't allowed into the hospital, but in the morning a nurse collected me from the wagon, which I'd parked out the back of the hospital so I could keep an eye on his stuff and his horse.

'The hospital staff refused to let Rocky go home without someone being there to help him when he arrived there ... and that's where we've both lived ever since.

'Home, in those days, was that old cottage which you no doubt saw when your family first arrived at Rocky's property. I still spend some time living there, but now consider my home to be upstairs in that barn close to the main house.'

'So, you became his housekeeper?'

'No. No way. We each look after our own residence, so to speak, unless he's crook, which isn't very often. Rocky's a tough old bugger and more like a father to me.

'Tell me more about that later mate,' I gently interrupted, 'I want to know how you speak the Queen's English better than I do.

'But I'm also curious how Rocky came to own such a fantastic acreage ... and that beautiful house. Max and Elspeth never mentioned anything about Rocky's finances; I'm confident they never knew about his true domestic situation.'

'Just the short version for now,' Adam answered, just a little impatiently, 'we're running out of time and besides, it's best if *you* get Rocky to explain things. Get him alone and ask him; he won't bite your head off.

'Right, first things first; the property. Rocky has always liked to gamble, cards in particular. Well, he got really lucky one night, and the loser had to forfeit just about everything he owned, not only the title to the land, but to the house which he'd built ... and the twenty or so cattle that remained on the property. The police were also onto that bloke who they suspected was rustling cattle and sheep, so he left the district rather smartly, never to be seen again.

'As for my English, well, Rocky insisted I get a better education and sponsored me to attend Melbourne University, which I did, and received an honours degree in Business Management. But that's it for now, we've got work to do.'

A new, even greater respect for Adam settled easily upon me.

11

———————

Mid-afternoon we reached our destination, The Dargo High Plains.

As we exited the scribbly snow gum timber which fringed the relatively flat and open terrain ahead of us, two things immediately impressed me. First, the altitude which afforded magnificent views of the blue-grey mountain ranges surrounding us, all partially hidden in the distance by a combination of eucalypt oil, and heat haze. And second, the feeling of remoteness.

Though it was a sunny day, an invigoratingly cold south-easterly wind was at work, pushing rafts of whitish grey clouds to some unknown end.

'Our *friends* should be waiting for us not far from here,' Adam announced quietly, 'but first we need to re-attach our lead ropes; we don't want one of those scoundrels getting too interested in either our packhorses, or what's in our saddlebags, or both.'

Having remounted, we unhurriedly walked our horses, it being clear that Adam wanted more time to offer me valuable advice. 'Most of the blokes you'll soon meet are from the Dorrigo region of New South Wales: that's a couple of hundred miles north of Sydney. They're all crooks, either on the run from the police and wanting to make a quick quid or two before moving on, or risking doing what they did at Dorrigo before new State Laws allowing police and graziers to shoot on sight made it too risky for them to stay. Just checking, but have you got one up the spout of that six shooter?'

'I have indeed,' I replied now just a bit apprehensive about what awaited us. 'Which I assume means all of *our friends* will be armed.'

'Most likely yes Leon, but not so the blacks if that gives you any comfort. There should be four or five of them. Leave them to me, I'll soon work out where their alliances lay.'

'So, what's their role in all this?'

'Basically, they'll become carriers. The cattle which'll be purchased from us today, will be moved closer to where they'll be slaughtered, then the meat will be carried by those black fellas to a "marginally honest" butcher operating in a small settlement called Grant ... from where he then services the needs all those working the nearby gold fields, at highly inflated prices of course. That meat transfer is done in the middle of the night, for reasons I'm sure you can understand.

'These blokes are operating under very specific instructions from Rocky and know the consequences if they don't deliver what he wants.'

'How so?' I replied in all innocence. 'Who gets paid and by who?'

Adam suddenly called a halt. 'OK Leon, you've a right to know,' he said, a serious tone to his voice. 'Listen carefully and *do not* discuss what I'm about to tell you with anyone other than either Rocky, or me. Do I have your word on this?'

'Absolutely.' We then shook hands.

'What you must realise Adam is that all the cattle you'll soon see don't strictly belong to Rocky. There will be two yarding's.

'The smaller yard will hold unbranded older cows only, those destined for the butcher at Grant. They'll all die never having felt a branding iron.

'The larger yard will hold a mix of a dozen cows with calves at foot; not all of them branded. These will be returning to Rocky's property with us. He'll have arranged for his brand to be applied as necessary as soon as we get home, thereby immediately rendering them as *his stock* which he can sell legally and without suspicion.

'Mind you Leon, all the cattle you see here were never Rocky's, but those of other graziers too lazy to prevent them from wandering off their leases.

'By the way, a twenty-fifth animal will be joining us, which I'll select this arvo. But I'll need you to give me a hand; OK?'

'A bull I suppose?' I interrupted, ever so wisely.

'Oooh no, it'll be an old cow who knows the way home; her name's Polly,' Adam replied while smiling smugly. 'One I've used on several previous musters: a trusted leader. And she's why dogs aren't needed; you'll see.'

'I'll explain more later, OK?'

'Hang on Adam, when do these blokes get paid?'

'As soon as the last beast leaves the yards.'

'So, that means you're carrying a hell of a lot of money,' I conjectured. 'A bit risky, isn't it?'

'Hell no, Leon. No risk at all, the money's in *your* saddle bags.'

* * *

WE SOON SIGHTED a group of six white men in the near distance sitting around a fire. As we approached, they all stood and stepped apart, quickly increasing their distance between each other. They were all armed; long-arms at the ready, albeit held in non-threatening poses.

'Well look at what the ugly black cat just dragged in,' said the chap who stepped forward in a blatant display of intended authority. He was about six feet tall and well-built if you ignored his beer gut, probably in his late forties, scruffily dressed, sporting not too many teeth, and repeatedly tugged on the end of his rather huge beard as if trying to convey wisdom, but instead obviously heralded an innate lack of trust. I immediately had him tagged as a smart-arse.

'Nice to see you again too, young Mickey,' Adam said confidently and cheerfully, 'but by the Jeezus you've put on a bit of flab since we last met.'

Before Mickey could respond to Adam's gently barbed greeting, Adam turned away slightly in his saddle, ignoring him, then threw open his arms to a now chuckling audience.

'Great to see you boys, thanks for being on time. And you can put down your guns; there's no need for 'em whatsoever. Anyway, I'd like you all to meet Leon, he's a relative of Rocky and is as keen as mustard.

'Now, how about a cuppa, we're parched. Make yourselves known to the lad; he won't bite.'

After handshakes all round, I sat on a block of snow-gum conveniently positioned close to the fire and from where I could keep an eye on our horses. These men, a disparate collection of different ages, builds, and work clothes, made me feel welcome: except for the smart-arse, Mickey, who couldn't resist pointing out my inexperience and belittling me at every opportunity.

Comfortingly, the others all seemed to have bright dispositions and were on for a yarn and a good laugh.

For some weeks of late, I'd been secretly comparing my build to Adam, and now realized I almost matched both his height and physique. Nevertheless, by this stage I had had a gut full of Mickey's persistent goading, and on an impulse, I stood and walked purposefully over to him and stopped directly in front him, occupying his space, and towering over him.

'You've crossed a line mate,' I said calmly, yet tinged with challenge as I removed my gun belt and handed it to the chap nearest to me. 'Now stand-up Mickey; we have a few differences which we obviously need resolving.

'For starters, I've never met you before today and I've done nothing to antagonize you since we met here, today. Does it get under your skin that Adam's in charge here, not you? Or is it that you reckon you can take out your pitiful grievances on me; you know, like give me a hiding while Adam's talking with his black mates over there?

'In either case that's offensive and I won't cop that. So, come on

Mickey, let's see what you've got. An apology would be a good start and save you considerable physical discomfort, or I'd be glad to teach you a few manners; take your pick.'

Mickey's first move was to quickly reach for his handgun, but it really wasn't his day. His bravado melted when the bloke sitting next to him grabbed his wrist and twisted it sharply to one side. I daresay the shotgun muzzle then pointing unwaveringly at his face also had something to do with Mickey's change of heart.

'It'd give me great pleasure to pull the trigger you bloody idiot. Apologize, and keep a civil mouth in future. Go on, piss off and cool down,' said the bloke sitting on the other side of Mickey.

Mickey rose slowly to his feet and staggered away accompanied by a volley of raucous laughter. He looked back once, his face distorted with humiliation, frustration, and a look which unmistakably foreshadowed that this encounter was not over and was now likely to end in someone's death.

I was in the process of buckling up my gun belt, wondering whether Adam had seen this piece of theatre being played out; he had.

'That went well,' he said cheerfully as he sat on the block of wood vacated by Mickey. 'Thanks for intervening you two, though it might have been an entertaining stoush. I'll have a word with him and let him know he's got one last chance to pull his head in. If he continues to provoke any of you, I'll send him packing.

'Anyway, I think the sooner we get this muster under way the better. I want to be on the move no later than an hour after dawn. You'll all be paid the agreed amount before we depart, and after that, well, good luck ... and no idle chatting to strangers, or spreading rumours or doing anything stupid that might bring the cops snooping around. You all know the consequences; yes?'

'Thanks again boys,' said Adam as he stood up and went from man to man shaking their hand. 'Righto, c'mon Leon, we've an old girl to find and to convince she needs to show us the way home.'

We collected our horses, and Adam led the way through the stunted alpine snow gum trees for about two hundred yards. We eventually arrived at a smallish, but very well-hidden clearing which contained two heavy-duty post and rail holding yards ... and twenty-four curious faces.

I followed suit as Adam dismounted, but then froze. Standing not more than fifteen feet in front of me were five very black men. I had not seen them as we approached the yards, nor had I heard them approach.

'Easy Leon, these boys are my close friends and are aware of who you are. And they saw you stand up to that nut case.'

Adam quickly introduced me to each of them, though I doubted if I'd remember their names. 'Now Leon, come over to the rails and tell me what you think of this bunch of beasties, and then we'll have a sit down with my brothers and have a good yarn.

'By the way, this is when they get paid; I'm not tempting fate, but it's best they decide what to do with their wages before others get a chance to exploit them.'

'To my eyes, mate, *Rocky's cattle* appear to be in tip-top condition and seem pretty relaxed.'

'But by tomorrow morning they'll be hungry and thirsty,' Adam replied with just a tint of excitement, 'and that's when you'll see how valuable Polly is. She knows exactly where to go for a feed and where the nearest creeks are located, all of which are conveniently in the direction we need to go to get home. The others will follow; you'll see.'

12

It was pleasant chatting with Adam's black brethren, though he had to act as interpreter. About an hour later, Adam stood and said something which made it clear he genuinely appreciated their help. A lot of head nodding, and smiles followed. They then all nodded to me in affirmation that I was now a kindred brother. (Well, that's what Adam told me later that day.)

'There's no need to look back,' he said, 'they've already made themselves scarce, and won't resurface until that other mob of cattle arrive at the place near Grant, I told you about. Let's hope we get to meet them all again next year.'

* * *

It didn't take us long to locate Polly for her almost white colour was in stark contrast to most of the green and brown surrounding vegetation. 'She's got a bit of age on her; at least ten years I reckon,' Adam said somewhat philosophically. 'We'll have to start thinking about her replacement, she can't go on for ever.'

Polly came to hand quickly enough, encouraged by the handful of rock salt which Adam magically produced for her. Getting her back to the yards was uneventful and she showed no reluctance to join her soon to be travel companions.

However, when we returned to the campfire to join the others for a cuppa, it was immediately evident a pall of unease still existed between the men. Mickey sat well apart from the others, a rifle laying across his thighs and a surly, threatening look contorted his face.

'What's got under your skin this time?' Adam asked reasonably.

'I'm sick of you and that little shit who thinks he's so damn good; and this lot aren't the sharpest knives in the drawer either. I want me pay, and I want it now!'

'Relax Mickey,' Adam said cheerfully, albeit deliberately ignoring his unjustified taunts. 'By the jeezus, mate, you're a bloody slow learner. You'll get your pay as agreed previously and not before ... and that's when the last of your mob of cattle leave the yards tomorrow morning. Spend it however you like, but not until you deliver that mob.

'If you shirk it, word'll get back to Rocky soon enough and you'll regret you were ever born. You know how he operates Mickey.'

I suddenly realised with somewhat of a shock there was a lot more to Rocky than I had previously thought. Those words undeniably conveyed the promise of certain death for betrayal.

Mickey, now fuming from Adam's advice, abruptly stood just as I dismounted, my back then facing him. Believing that Adam had matters under control, I listened with a smile on my face to another tirade of abuse from Mickey.

Suddenly, Adam's voice boomed. 'You bloody fool, Mickey, put that gun down this instant.'

'Or what? you interfering black bastard.'

A shiver gripped my spine but then suddenly jolted me into action. I spun, at the same time pushing myself as hard and as quickly as I could away from my horse, hoping I might avoid getting shot—and while in the process—come up with a means of helping Adam. I lost my balance while desperately trying to release my six-shooter from its holster and fell ignominiously onto my knees and empty hands. Nobody was laughing.

In the process of standing, I again stumbled, but then froze: the air was suddenly filled with a strange *whah, whah, whah, whah* sound, accompanied soon after by a blur of movement, a solid thump, and a scream of pain ... then, a single rifle shot!

'God Almighty, are you OK Leon?' Adam shouted, obviously concerned as he jogged over to me.

'Yeah, I'm Ok, but did anyone get shot?'

'Nah, his rifle accidentally discharged ... a reflex action I reckon; he was out like a light before he hit the ground. Thankfully that shot went wide; but it must have missed you by only a cat's whisker.'

'So, what happened to Mickey, he looks dead to me?'

'He'll probably live, Jimmies boomerang hit him simultaneously on the shoulder and the side of his head. He's gunna have a hell of a headache for a few days. Serves the bastard right.

'Here Leon, have you seen one of these things before? It's called a boomerang, and it just saved your life, and mine too I suspect.'

'I've heard about 'em, but never handled one; so, where did it come from!?'

'Why not ask the bloke standing behind you?'

I turned, and there, barely a yard away stood one of Adam's, no, *our*, brothers. Jimmie was his name, as best as I could recall.

Smiling broadly, he reached for the return of his weapon.

I intended to oblige, but hesitated, holding it firmly at one end. With both of us now holding the boomerang, I gently pulled it back toward me, and as hoped, Jimmie followed. With our free hands we shook, then smiled, and nodded in mutual understanding. I then released his weapon, but not the need to one day repay a debt.

'Nicely handled Leon,' Adam said quietly as we watched Jimmie disappear into the snow gum tree line carrying his boomerang.

'Thanks, but I still have no idea why Mickey has had me in his sights; I did nothing whatsoever to upset the man. But I don't want him to die, so we'd best try and make him comfortable for the night.'

'He's always had a huge chip on his shoulders, right from the day I first met him,' Adam replied thoughtfully. 'Rocky's certain he's an alcoholic. I do too, but I reckon something else must have scrambled his brain when he was a youngster. Abusive parents always threatening and depriving him, perhaps.'

'Yes', I replied after a few seconds of reflection, 'that could do it.'

We dragged Mickey closer to the fire, rolled him into his swag and covered his torso with both of his blankets. There was a decent sized bruise forming on his right cheek bone, in the space between the corner of his eye, and his temple.

As I gently lifted Mickey's head and placed it onto his pillow, I noticed a nearly dry trickle of blood had almost found its way into his ear: that could be cleaned up tomorrow, provided he didn't cark it overnight.

In the meantime, his vital signs of life were strong, if his apparently contented snoring was any guide.

13

____

To my surprise, when I awakened before dawn the next morning, the campfire had been fed back into life and both Adam and Mickey were sitting together enjoying a cuppa, and hopefully each other's company. Both had rolled up their swags, so, I dressed quickly and followed suit.

I poured myself a brew, threw in a handful of sugar and joined them, sitting so that Mickey was between me and Adam. 'Good morning,' I said as cheerfully as the early hour called for, 'how's your head mate? You sure had us worried last night; that was a nasty blow you copped.'

Mickey slowly turned his head in my direction, I daresay to give me a close look at his injury. In the flickering light of the campfire, his face, though not contorted in malice, was yet an ugly, scary sight to behold. His left eye was completely closed, and the entire left-hand side of his face was swollen hideously, making him almost unrecognisable.

'Yes, it was, but I'll live,' Mickey stammered, the swelling of his face making it difficult to understand what he was saying. 'An me shoulder's bloody killin' me.' That having been said, he stood up, threw the dregs of his tea onto the fire, picked up his swag and walked off.

'I've tried talking some sense into him,' Adam said quietly, 'but I doubt it; he still doesn't believe the world isn't out to get at him; his words basically, not mine. Anyway, I've paid him and if he's got any decency left in him, he'll do his job.

'OK Leon let's cook the last of our bacon and eggs and get the rest of these blokes up and about. They should be keen enough, it's their payday after all.'

* * *

An hour later we all met at the cattle holding yards. 'Righto boys, come and get your pay.'

That done, Adam walked to the yard gate and threw it wide open. 'Now you lot, get these beauties moving before they die of old age. And remember to give 'em time to get a good drink and some pickings under their belts before yah start movin' 'em on hard, like. Good luck, and not a word to anyone; got it!'

Man, and beast were all soon out of sight, the only indication of their existence being the occasional bellow, receding in volume, as the mob moved away and down into one of the valleys confronting them.

'Our turn now Leon. First, I'll get into the yard and move Polly up to the gate, then you swing the gate wide open,' Adam instructed. 'Just make sure you keep well out of the way; they'll all probably want to be first out after Polly. Anyway, no need to shut the gate after them.'

Within ten minutes, Polly had picked up the home trail and her adopted mob were enthusiastically following her.

* * *

With only one exception, the trail was downhill, so by midday our mob had made good progress.

'That clearing where this track first crosses the Buckland is only about a mile from here, so we'll stop there and give the calves a decent rest,' Adam announced. 'And I could do with a cuppa or two, and the last of our barley sugar. What do you say Leon?'

About fifteen minutes later we arrived at that clearing. It was amazing to watch the cattle circling the open ground looking for a pick of grass, and for a place where they could breast the river for a drink as if Polly had read Adam's mind and she was passing on our thoughts to her mob.

'Well, I'll be buggered,' cried Adam, breaking my daydreaming, 'look who's come to meet us.'

14

———

Approaching us from the opposite side of the river were three riders: Rocky, Max ... and Fay. By the time our welcoming party crossed the river, I had a fire going and the billy on the boil. I'd also retrieved from my saddle bags all the makings for a much-needed cuppa, plus the remaining few pieces of my barley sugar.

'G'day, g'day boys', Rocky cheerfully shouted his greeting while waving his hat, obviously relieved and I daresay glad to see we had not only safely made it this far, but on schedule and with all thirteen head accounted for. Max likewise looked excited, his face beaming a combination of relief and pride, I suspected.

And there was Fay, wearing men's working clothes, boots and a wide brimmed hat which failed to restrain her blond hair; her face even more beautiful than I had been trying to recall, though it was only a few days since we parted.

As Adam walked past me to greet our guests, albeit much closer than was necessary, he hesitated, then whispered to me. 'Pick up your jaw mate, before you get a gob full of blowflies. Keep your wits about you, and look after that beautiful girl, or I'll be looking for her attentions myself.'

That was the jolt of reality I needed. I tried to reply, but my mouth was as dry as a dead gum leaf. Besides, Adam had moved on, chuckling to himself.

As soon as Rocky and my stepfather dismounted, Adam first shook Rocky's hand and then Max's.

Fay however, at first seemed reluctant to dismount, but when I arrived beside her horse, any inhibitions she may have been suppressing, vanished. In one athletic movement she swung from her saddle and landed in my arms. We hugged with unexpected urgency, then separated and gazed into each other's eyes. That was it: I was smitten.

Yes, we then kissed, much longer than was perhaps acceptable, however, a discreet cough from Max who witnessed all of this from just a few yards away, put an end to that incredible first kiss.

'I'd like to have a talk with you two,' Max said quietly, without any bitterness, 'but not until we've had a cuppa, eh?' I unhanded Fay (reluctantly, I recall) and jogged over to the fireplace to finalise the tea making ritual.

In the meantime, Adam, Rocky, Max and Fay walked amongst the cattle, discussing each individual bovine's attributes, and estimating their current worth at market.

As I started pouring the tea, the others joined me and sat on a convenient log not far from the fire. I then passed around the sugar bag and handed out the last of my barley sugar. When I was about to take up my position on the log, Max stood and moved, leaving me a place to sit so that we would be sitting either side of Fay.

Conversation and some laughter ebbed and flowed, then Rocky said, 'I haven't got much time for Mickey, but I can't fault his selection of quality animals. And just look at Polly, she's looking bloody good for her age, I reckon she might still have a couple of years left in her.'

Adam then delivered a condensed version of our successful high-country muster, but when he'd finished, conversation turned to Mickey's strange behaviour. 'I hope that's the last we see of him,' Rocky said candidly, 'he's become a liability which could see all of us landing in jail if we're not bloody careful.' Which now meant Max, and Fay, and probably Elspeth were also in Rocky's employ.

* * *

BY THIS STAGE, all the cattle were lying down and contentedly chewing their cud, while Rocky and Adam were now sitting side by side leaning against a log, engaged in earnest discussion.

Max then stood and gestured for Fay and me to follow him. We walked about forty yards downstream, along the top of the riverbank, then we all sat, taking in the river's peaceful babbling, the various bird calls, an orchestra of buzzing insects and the gentle rustle of the leaves in the overhead tree canopies created by a gentle, refreshing north easterly breeze.

A few minutes passed during which not a word was spoken. Unexpectedly, Max broke the silence. 'Elspeth and I have discussed you two at length. Leon, you've been blind for some time; not noticing Fay's efforts to engage with her; perhaps that's because, from day one, you've accepted her as "just your little sister".

'Fay, even at your young age, you have wisdom beyond any man's understanding, for which you should be proud.

'From the day we decided to migrate to Australia, you've both grown rather rapidly, both physically and your outlook on life ... particularly in the past six months or so.

'There are no blood ties between you both, so we see no reason why nature should not take its natural course ... which is why we're having this chat. Life in our adopted country can be a bit rough around the edges, as you have no doubt both noticed. Our only wish is that if you see a life together ahead of you, then look after each other, and always be truthful and understanding.

'I realise this sounds like a sermon, but Elspeth and I are very proud of you both and extend our very best wishes, whichever way you wish to live your lives from this point on. But, please, don't be strangers to us, for we pledge to always be your sounding board. And your protectors where we can.'

Max stood, put a hand on each of our shoulders, squeezed gently then walked away.

Head spinning from Max's words, I turned to look at Fay who had wiggled along the edge of the riverbank to be sitting right beside me. Up that close, I noticed the freckles on her cheeks for the first time. Then, our eyes met.

15

———

'Come on you two, we've got work to do,' Adam called, breaking that precious moment of intimacy.

We walked back to the campfire, hand-in-hand, but Adam glared at me and said, 'We haven't got all day, so please gather up your horses and repack, we've got to get a move on. I'll fill you in on things as we head home.'

By now, Rocky and Max had roused our mob from their cud-chewing and daydreaming by dropping several handfuls of salt on the opposite side of the river. Once the cattle got a whiff of the salt, there was a collective rush and jockeying to be first across. In just a few minutes the salt disappeared, and long strings of saliva now hung from the mouths of most beasts, calves included.

Though Fay and I followed the mob across the river, there was no need for us to push the cattle on. Already, Polly was in leisurely pursuit of Rocky and Max, who by then, were about two hundred yards down the track spreading a few more mounds of salt.

Another mile further on, Adam returned to the rear of the mob and positioned his horse in between my, and Fay's mounts. 'Rocky has another job teed up for me and you, Leon. As soon as we've reprovisioned and packed, we're to head off, tomorrow like. It seems

Rocky received a note from the bloke who lives on a remote station and would appreciate an opportunity to discuss what appears to be *strange goings on.*

'Rocky's written back to him and wants us to deliver his reply; he can't do that trip; his leg's been giving him buggery. But it seems the matter's reasonably urgent, so we're off again. Rocky wouldn't respond if he didn't trust this bloke.

'His name's Jim Barclay. Rocky and I met him once, not long after he'd moved into the station sometime during middle of sixteen, not the warmest time of the year to be moving in.

'Anyway, he's not a bad sort of bloke. He was employed by the property owners as the Wonnangatta Station manager and usually lives there alone; mind you he hasn't been there a year yet, like.

'That station's about twenty-five miles from our place, and we'll probably be gone for two nights. We'll be using the same horses; they weren't worked hard on this muster and should still be fresh enough. Mind you, we'll be following a couple of different tracks which I've only used twice before. It's ruggedly beautiful country, but so steep in places we'll have to walk. It's tough going, but we can do it.

'According to the stories told to me by my aboriginal foster parents, when I was just a young 'un, like, I believe where we're going is my mob's traditional country,' Adam said casually. 'They were known as the Pengerang, Minjambuta, Duduroa and Jaitmathang peoples who spoke the Waywurra, Mogullumibidj and Dhudhuroa languages.

Smiling at the unusual way Adam proudly pronounced these strange words, I replied cheekily, 'That's easy for you to say mate.'

Adam turned to look at me, never said a word initially, but gradually the look of irritation on his face was replaced by a huge smile. We three then burst into raucous laughter which challenged the best efforts of a local kookaburra family.

'I'll help you pack, but I won't tag along,' said Fay once normality returned. 'I've promised to help Elspeth with a few jobs that need doing.'

In my ignorance of the ways and needs of womenfolk, I was

surprised and disappointed by her firm response but consoled myself quickly enough knowing we'd be apart for only two days.

Upon arriving back at Rocky's property, the mob were yarded in the paddock nearest to the house.

Elspeth greeted us warmly, but my stepbrothers Bertie and Paul couldn't have cared less being intent upon climbing the post and rail fence and throwing stones at the cattle. To his credit, Max dragged them off the fence and gave them both a clip behind their ears, then yelled, 'Now get inside. I'll talk to you two later.

'Oh, by the way,' Max said, quickly composed, and now all business-like, 'if it's OK with you two gentlemen, I'll be staying here. I've already given Elspeth my word to help her with some heavy lifting.'

'All good mate,' Adam replied. 'We'll be back soon enough, then we'll give you a hand; right Leon?'

* * *

As agreed, I met Adam in the kitchen before dawn. To my surprise, Elspeth was already up, cooking eggs and bacon, and to my even greater surprise, Fay was pouring coffee for us both ... a real treat. Toast and honey were also on the menu, served just as Rocky joined us. It never ceases to amaze me how country folk can surface, wide awake and always cheerful. Mind you, on this occasion, excitement was in the air for an adventure of sorts which was about to get underway.

An hour later, the horses had been brought up to the house, saddled, swags attached and both packhorses loaded.

'I'm assuming you both have your guns and enough ammo?' Rocky asked. 'Just in case you don't, here's another box.

'You should know the tracks to follow well enough Adam, but still, keep your wits about you. I dunno why, but I've got a strange feeling in me waters that all's not as it should be. Jim's an accomplished bushman I do believe, and an honest bloke, but he's on his own as best I know ... and just might need some kind of support up there.

'You remember when we met him, eh Adam? He was intending to employ a cook and a general farmhand and mentioned a bloke named Bamford, John Bamford. We both know that supposed *gentleman* and warned Jim off employing him.'

'Why's that?' I asked, genuinely interested.

'Well, Leon,' Rocky continued, 'there's a bloody good chance Bamford murdered his wife, and, he's known to be easily provoked, even in jest, and has a violent temper. And, from our experience, we've known him to boast about how easily he can steal cattle, whether branded or not.'

'A nasty piece of work,' I replied earnestly. 'Sounds to me as if he's cut from the same piece of cloth as that mad bastard, Micky. Surely Jim could've been a bit more selective?'

'It wouldn't surprise me and Adam that those two are in fact well known to each other and probably in cahoots. But, don't let's underestimate Jim,' Rocky replied evenly, 'there's bloody few honest and hardworking workers around now because of the war, so Jim's choices were pretty damn limited.

'Anyway, good luck boys. Enjoy the ride and give my best regards to Jim.'

Adam mounted, then Rocky handed him the lead rope for his packhorse.

I was about to follow suit, but I never had a hope; Fay was all over me. 'Take care, Leon, my love.'

We kissed and hugged, perhaps just a wee bit too passionately for this time of the day, then I swung up into my saddle, leatherwork creaking as the stirrups took my weight.

The mid-December dawn air was cool, and although a light mist had settled, the first rays of the sun were just caressing the neighbouring mountain peaks. And yes, as we left the house yard, of course I waved and blew air kisses intended only for Fay.

Almost immediately after we kicked our horses into a leisurely canter, we startled a mob of kangaroos and were simultaneously treated to the first peals of laughter from a family of local kookaburras welcoming this new, potentially warm day.

16

After two days of traversing some very steep and sometimes treacherous terrain, Adam called a halt. We left the horses to rest and to browse, and we soon had the billy boiling.

'Like I said,' Adam reflected, 'that was always going to be tough, but it gets a lot easier now. We've only got about a mile to go. Same drill as before, make sure your guns are loaded, and that you've got one up the spout.

* * *

Close to midday, Adam led the way into the southern extremity of a substantial high plains clearing, then we headed north. 'You'll see Jim's hut and his yards in a few minutes. I dunno how some folks can survive in such remote places, even if the pay was good.'

'It must be possible though,' I replied. 'Your ancestors did, somehow.'

We crested a small rise and gazed upon a small and rustic building with nearby post and rail stockyards on both sides. There was no smoke coming from the chimney, and no sign of Jim or his horse, or horses ... and no sight of any cattle whatsoever.

But, when we got within thirty or so yards of the hut, a dog barked a healthy challenge, albeit emanating from a hideout somewhere towards the rear of the hut. We both called out for Jim several times but got no response, so we let ourselves in. The dog went quiet.

The interior was unexpectedly tidy. In the kitchen, pots and pans were suspended from overhead hooks, the quite large fireplace was without any ashes, the kitchen sink was clean, the adjoining benches were spotless and uncluttered, and a non-perishables food cupboard was well stocked. Curiously, the words "home tonight" were etched in chalk on the back of the kitchen door.

'Hey Adam, look in here, quick!'

'I think this must 'ave been Jim's room. Not so tidy, eh? Looks to me as if there was a fight of sorts in here. And look, there's a shotgun; pass it to me please Leon.

Adam broke the shotgun and sniffed its firing chamber. 'It's been fired, and recently. Here, you have a whiff.'

There was no doubting Adam's assessment. 'I can't see any blood-stains anywhere though. Perhaps we shouldn't read too much into that, but there's a goddamn scary feeling about what's happened here, eh?'

'Yeah, that's for sure,' Adam said as we exited that room. 'I was looking in the other room before you called me: Bamford's, I do believe. Almost as dishevelled, and most of his belongings are missing. No clothes, no saddle, no bridle and... '

'And no horse outside as we've already seen,' I chimed in.

'As much as I dislike talking with the police, at some stage we're going to have to report this, but not until we fill Rocky in.

'See if you can find anything for that dog while I have a quick scout around outside.'

All that I could find was some dry biscuits and a chunk of hard cheese. Not ideal, but it would have to suffice.

Adam indicated where I could find the dog, not a bad type as it turned out, but right then he was obviously very hungry judging by how quickly he gave up his hideout to wolf down that meagre meal.

17

'There's no sign of cattle having been down this way recently, which is quite concerning,' Adam said confidently, then continued. 'Regardless, we must search for Jim, he might be in a spot of bother. And brace yourself for bad news.

'Look, you take this side of the creek, and I'll cross over. Give a shout occasionally and try to keep in sight of each other.'

We secured our pack horses into a side yard then quickly mounted our usual horses. They responded well even though they'd worked hard over the past two days.

About half a mile along, I reined in. The ground was dry and dusty and was not only littered with many cattle tracks and reasonably fresh droppings ... but also the distinct hoof prints of at least two horses.

I was about to dismount for a closer inspection when I heard Adam hailing me. I turned my horse in the direction from where I thought Adam had called, sunk in my heels, and was soon galloping towards the creek.

I soon found Adam, and the most likely cause of a smell which had pervaded the air since our arrival at this remote station. He stood leaning against his horse, about twenty feet away from a body; clearly a very dead person given the hordes of blow flies all vying to ensure their next generation.

'Jim Barclay?' I asked solemnly, unintentionally stating the obvious. Adam looked at me and nodded.

'Murdered?'

'Yep; shot in the back at close range with a shotgun, no less.'

'Who the bloody hell would do this?'

'You've already answered that. My money's on that demented bastard, Mickey.'

'Why him?'

'Well Leon, there are some very useful things I've inherited, you know, like tracking. There's no doubt in my mind those hoof prints belong to that bay waler which belongs to Mickey.

'Remember when we were mustering last week? Well, one of the things I instinctively do is make a mental note of which horse belongs to who. And I do the same with human footprints.

'Right now, I swear that both the hoof prints and those boot marks belong to non-other than Mickey.

'And don't forget he had a shotgun with him.'

I stared at the ground. Hoofprints were plain to see, but Adam had to identify the boot marks for me.

'Leon, we can't just leave Jim lying here, we've got to bury him and quickly. Every minute we spend doing that puts us further behind those two mongrels; I'm convinced Mickey and Bamford are in cahoots.'

'By the way, just before you called me earlier on, I'd not only come across heaps of cattle tracks, but among them there were definitely two sets of horse hoof prints.'

Adam looked at me, nodded and said quietly, 'Good work Leon, that's exactly what I expected.'

Back at the hut, it didn't take us long to find a mattock and a shovel.

We also soon discovered how hard the ground was, which made digging extremely difficult. 'OK, that's going to be good enough, Adam soon decided, 'we'll just have to cover his body with rocks. You start gathering some while I get his body into this scrape we've dug.' In hindsight, that was a very generous suggestion on Adam's behalf.

About an hour later when Jim's shallow grave was completed, we rode back to the hut. Having returned the tools to their rightful place, Adam walked down to the creek, stripped off and plunged into the creek.

Realising that I too was probably on the nose, I followed suit. Before heading back to the hut, we both gave our clothes and socks a thorough wash.

Back at the hut we dressed in dry and clean clothes and socks, then set about loading the packhorses. 'We've still got several hours of daylight left,' Adam said determinedly. 'Let's hang our wet stuff to dry inside the hut, then let's get after those bastards. But first, we'd better see if there's any food for the dog. We'll collect him and our clothes on the way home.'

We'd travelled about a mile before Adam turned in his saddle and said, 'You do realise Leon that we're being followed?'

I spun around expecting the worst, but there was Jim's dog tagging along about ten yards behind our packhorses, tail wagging and smiling at us.

* * *

WITHIN THE NEXT FEW MINUTES, we had traversed the cleared land known officially as The Wonnangatta Station. The cloven cattle tracks were simple enough to follow, a herd of twenty or so beasts held in close formation leave a significant amount of turned and trodden earth.

The track was generally much less steep and easier to ride compared to that we had navigated on our approach to Jim's property. Accordingly, we were making good time and to my surprise, it wasn't long before Adam called a halt. 'Well, what do yah know,' he said sarcastically. 'Two mobs have become one, and not long ago if I'm not mistaken.

'OK, Leon,' Adam said, 'make sure you've got one up the spout, and if I'm also not mistaken, it's only an hour or so before we'll arrive at those holding yards I've told you about; they're located roughly half a mile this side of the Grant settlement.

'C'mon mate, let's push on, there's still at least two hours of daylight left. To limit being seen we'll camp outside of Grant.'

We both gently heel-tapped our horse's ribs while gathering our reins; it was no surprise that our walers walked off shoulder to shoulder and at a good clip. However, to our mutual surprise, Jim's dog was now purposefully leading us.

18

———

The camp site chosen by Adam was off the main track, well concealed from view, supplied with ample shade, and served by a small, crystal-clear creek. The only reservation I had was the stench of humanity which, it seemed, descended upon us every time there was a wind change.

'Right, now Leon,' Adam said suddenly, seeking my attention. 'I'm going walkabout to see if I can locate some of my brothers. I've got a strong feeling they won't be far from here. However, it's best that I go alone, they'll be more relaxed about telling me about what's going on in Grant, who's arrived recently, and so on.

'Don't wait up for me mate; get your dinner whenever you want... and feed our dog. And have a think about a good name for him: something fitting like.'

With that said, Adam departed.

* * *

THERE WAS plenty of wood lying about, and it took me only a few minutes to get a fire going. The dog made me chuckle during this time; without any instruction, he not only selected a reasonably hefty branch, but carried it back to the camp site and dropped it close to the fire. *'Ehm, just like a lumberjack,'* I thought. *'Nah, too long, how about simply, "Jack."'*

Just for fun, I called that name and patted my knee in the hope he might respond. And, as if to clinch the deal, the dog pricked his ears, trotted up to me and sat, leaning against my leg. *'Right, so Jack it is.'*

I fed Jack the last of my bacon and a slice of bread which disappeared in the blink of an eye. 'Strewth, you poor bugger, you really are starving. If the butcher in Grant is open, I'll get you something decent tomorrow. If not, I'll bowl over a wallaby, or a roo, OK?'

I swear to God, Jack seemed to know exactly what I said, responding with a single, muffled yap of acceptance.

Reminiscing, I realised that owning a dog like this would have been a major reason why Jim Barclay could manage the life of solitude he had chosen and would be just the sort of dog I'd love to have when I eventually owned my own property.

* * *

I NEVER HEARD Adam arrive back at our camp site, but the next morning when I awoke and poked my head clear of my swag, there, side by side sat Adam and Jack. As Adam fed sticks onto the growing fire, Jack followed his every movement as if supervising the process.

'Morning; when did you get back?', I asked sleepily, while propping myself up on my elbows. In just three bounds, Jack was all over me, licking my face and wriggling like a loon.

'About two-ish. Get dressed while the billy boils and we'll have a good chat: I've got some news that'll no doubt interest you.'

Having returned from the nearby scrub to satisfy a strong call to nature, I washed my hands and face: if I wasn't awake before, I was then, that water was bloody cold even though it was late December.

When I sat down next to the fire, Adam handed me a mug of sweetened black tea, and a plate of freshly cooked damper smothered with honey. 'There, get that into yah Leon,' he said jovially, 'but don't be expecting room service every morning.'

I was taking my first mouthful of damper and looked up. Adam was handing a chunk of damper to Jack.

'By the way, I've decided his name should be, Jack,' I said while yawning. 'What do you reckon?'

'I was thinking something more like Thesaurus.

'Nah, *Jack* is good.' Only then did Adam serve himself that which remained of the damper. 'Not a bad type, eh? He'd be an asset back home.'

We were onto our second mug of tea when Adam said, 'I was right, our brothers are camped only about half a mile from here.

'And we were also right about Jim's cattle being stolen. And, as we thought, that theft was timed to coincide with our mob being brought down from Hotham.

'All of those cattle are in those holding yards just up the road. Our bushranger friends will have their work cut out when I ask them to explain why half of them carry Rocky's brand.'

Adam paused to finish his cuppa, then said. 'Things get better, or worse I really mean. You remember Jimmie, the bloke who clobbered Micky with his boomerang?'

'How could I not, he bloody well saved my life.'

'Well, he and one of his mob overheard Mickey and Bamford talking about their plans before the robbery, and they witnessed everything after it got under way. Apparently, they had a perfect view from their vantage point'.

'Be buggered! Really?'

'Yep, they had nothing to lose by telling me everything, besides, they've both had nasty run-ins with both of those bastards.

'Go on, do tell. This should be very interesting; I'm all ears.'

'Well, Jimmy and that mate of his watched Micky and Bamford, and it wasn't long after Barclay's cattle were on the move that Barclay appeared, riding flat out after them. And it seems Jack here was with him.

'When Jim caught up to them, he immediately challenged Bamford. Jimmie couldn't hear what they were saying, but it was obvious a heated argument was in progress.

'Micky was leading the cattle and was probably unaware of what was taking place; the cattle were on top note letting it be known they were annoyed at being herded along with unfamiliar strangers.

'Anyway, Jim Barclay was doing a lot of shouting and pointing, but eventually he threw both his arms into the air, in disgust I expect, then wheeled his horse around and took off at a gallop back towards the hut. Whether Jim was not armed or became aware that Bamford was reaching for *his* shotgun ... I didn't learn. But it wasn't long before Bamford was racing after Jim.

'Not sure why, but Jim urged his horse to cross the creek, but it stumbled getting up the far bank, sending him arse over head out of his saddle and landing heavily. Jim, having recovered quickly, was desperately trying to get back into the saddle, but his horse was spooked and made it very tricky for Jim to do so.

'He never made it. That murdering bastard Bamford caught up, dismounted and without hesitation fired his shotgun straight into Jim's back from just a few yards away.

'Anyway, as Jim slumped to the ground, our newfound friend here attacked Bamford, full on, like. Grabbed an arm and started shaking it savagely.

'Lucky for Jack, the shotgun, as we know, is only single shot. Bamford tried to kick and then club Jack with the shotgun, but Jack was too quick—and smart—releasing his grip and took off to the hut leaving no time for Bamford to reload.

'Bamford followed Jack back to the hut but made no attempt to locate him. And note, when Bamford returned outside, he wasn't carrying the shotgun.

'As we know, Jim never had a handgun when we found him, which means Bamford knew his boss was unarmed; but that didn't stop him from shooting Jim in the back. That mongrel then rode away and joined Mickey help push the cattle towards Grant.'

'Not only a coward but a murderer to boot,' I recall saying, and then adding sincerely, 'so help me, Adam, I'm going to square the ledger with those rotten bastards, even if it takes a lifetime.

'And what about poor bloody Jack when we turned up at Jim's

hut? He must have been petrified thinking it was Bamford coming back to have another go at killing him!'

We both then went silent, realising our emotions needed to cool.

Ten minutes later, I sensed some impatience in Adam's mood. 'So, what do you have in mind doing for the rest of the day?' I asked quietly.

19

———————

s we rode towards Grant, Adam reiterated his plans ... just in case.

'Right, first, we'll pay a visit to the butcher's shop. But keep your eyes peeled for those two crims ... and make sure you've got one up the spout. Then we'll, "all friendly like", buy some meat for ourselves and something for Jack.

'When there's nobody else in the shop, we can start asking the proprietor a few questions and see what kind of a response we get. My guess is that if he's up to no good, he'll not be very welcoming.

'We don't want to come across as police, but being strangers, he'll be suspicious anyway. If he gets like that, we'll ask his advice about such as if we can buy a miner's license here, and whether there's a local boarding house.

'That *might* get him talking; we'll just have to wait and see. It's also my guess that he *will* object to me being black, so, Leon, you'll have to take the lead, OK?'

'Yeah, I think I can manage that.'

IT WAS HOT, and cicadas thrummed loudly in the overhead eucalypt canopies as we rode into Grant around midday, and it was abundantly clear many folks were living rough, given the very temporary appearance of their dwellings.

More people than I was expecting, mostly miners I guessed, were resting in the shade having their lunch, chatting, and nonchalantly swishing fronds of bracken at the determined, tormenting hordes of bushflies which surrounded them. Those folk on the move were unhurried and seemed friendly enough, and either waved, smiled, or nodded to us as we passed.

We dismounted, tethered our horses, and casually walked into the butcher's shop. The smell inside was woeful but could have been worse. One customer was departing, and we exchanged pleasantries, albeit briefly.

That left one customer being served and another standing back from the serving counter. We sidled up to that bloke intending to ask him a few questions, but abruptly, the butcher called, 'Next', I haven't got all day.'

The second customer took an inordinate time to make his selections, and a similar time to find the cash he needed; half of what he owed getting put on the slate to be paid next week. "Or else" was implied by the look of annoyance on the butcher's face.

Since entering the shop, the butcher's shifty glances in our direction did not go unnoticed.

'Next!' the butcher called again, then quickly added in a most derogative manner. 'I'm not serving no Abo, so, what do yah want young fella?'

'And a good day to you too, sir,' I replied evenly, 'My name's Leon, nice to meet you. We're just passing through, but do you have a choice of steak cuts available?'

'Son, this is a butcher shop, what do *you* reckon?'

'Yes, yes of course, I was just hoping for a decent couple of Scotch fillets, a dozen snags, and, oh yes, I'll need some bones and off-cuts for me dog.'

'Yes of course, but how do you intend to pay.'

'By cash, sir.'

'So, prove it! Slap twenty quid on the counter, or you can both piss off.'

'Of course, here you are. I'll make it twenty-five quid if you'll answer a few questions for me.' The butcher's head jerked up, his face a blend of the prospect of making a very lucrative, albeit lopsided deal, and his curiosity.

'Yeah, OK. What d'yah wanna know?'

I didn't reply immediately, for some inexplicable reason, instead, I glanced at the glass panel on the door which led to the rear of the shop. That glance probably saved my life ... for in that glass panel was the unmistakeable reflection of someone about to enter the shop from the street: none other than that murdering creep, Bamford!

I tossed my money on the counter, scooped up our meat bundle, turned and walked to where Adam was standing, hoping the view of my back would obstruct Bamford from recognising either of us.

That ploy worked. The shop was quite gloomy and the fact neither Adam nor I had shaved for the past week, both probably contributed to that success. (My first attempt at growing a beard, the fashion of those times.)

Bamford would have been aware of two other customers in the shop, but he pointedly ignored us. He aggressively strode up to the butcher, and yelled, 'You'd better have my meat ready to go mate, or I'll kick your lazy backside all the way down to Dargo.'

The butcher was visibly annoyed, but rallied gallantly and said, 'It's been ready since six this morning, just as you asked for it to be.'

'And it's paid for, right?' Bamford blustered, trying to big note himself.

I didn't wait for the butcher to respond to that bluff, or veiled threat; *now* was our opportunity seize the moment and nail Bamford!

Confident he was oblivious to my presence, I walked over, stood directly behind him and said loudly and confidently, 'Well, well, well, if it isn't John Bamford. Pray tell, you coward, why did you murder Jim Barclay?' He was defenceless as you well know.'

Initially, Bamford froze, but then quickly spun around, one hand moving swiftly towards his holster. There was both surprise and loathing on his face, which dramatically changed to shock when he realised that not only was his handgun missing ... but that he was now staring into its barrel, now only inches from his face.

Adam had expertly picked Bamford's pocket, so to speak, and by the look on Adams face, I was seriously worried about what he might do next.

'That's enough you lot, get out of my shop,' the butcher yelled, and to re-enforce his quite reasonable request, it was obvious there was no point arguing with his double-barrelled shotgun now levelled in our direction.

'Yah dopey bastard,' Bamford screamed at the butcher, 'go on, shoot these idiots, or it'll be your fault our plans get buggered up. Can't you see they're cops or bounty hunters for Christ's sake! Why do you reckon we've been paying yah so much? Earn yah keep; go on, shoot these bastards ... now!'

I think Adam must have read my mind: we weren't waiting for the butcher to obey Bamford's demand. I scooped up our meat package, and together Adam and I very smartly frog-marched Bamford outside and onto the boardwalk.

However, what we didn't anticipate was the menace presenting itself to us in the form of the rider dismounting next to our tethered horses: non-other this time, than Mickey, the demented idiot that only a week ago had damn nearly killed me!

Of course, Mickey no doubt recognised Bamford, and may have even identified our horses, but nevertheless he froze, unable I suspect, to immediately recognise either Adam, or me.

But he certainly recognised Bamford's predicament and was having none of it. In one fluid, unexpected movement, Mickey launched himself back into his saddle, gathered his reins, then yanked his horse's head around while furiously jabbing his heels into the horse's ribs.

Adam fired once but regrettably, missed.

Mickey's horse responded gallantly and when it was about five or six strides away at near full gallop, Mickey raised a two-finger salute, then swung in his saddle to face us and fired a single return shot.

That shot was to change my life for ever. It had to have been a fluke shot, but it was nevertheless lethal.

In that crazy moment, Adam died; that bullet entering the left side of his head, killing him instantly.

In disbelief, I sank to my knees beside Adam, unwittingly releasing my hold on Bamford. Ever the opportunist, Bamford sprinted to his horse, mounted, and took off at full gallop in the same direction Mickey had taken.

Anger unexpectedly replaced my disbelief. Without hesitation, I aimed my six-shooter and fired, regardless that Bamford's back was then my target.

Bamford lurched to his left and remained in that position. Obviously, I had enjoyed better luck, but it wasn't sufficient to bring him immediate grief or dislodge him. [Some months would pass before I learnt my shot had shattered Bamford's left elbow.]

'You rotten bastards!! Consider yourselves both dead men walking,' I screamed on top note as those two disappeared in a cloud of dust. My taunt was genuine, and I prayed that from this day, those two would forever be looking over their shoulders wherever they went.

I turned back to Adam, whose legs still twitched occasionally. Sadly, I sat beside him and gently lifted his head and shoulders onto my lap, unaware of the blood oozing from his head. At the realisation Adam had been snatched forever from this life, deep despair and nausea almost overwhelmed me.

'Go peacefully, my friend,' I mumbled through gut wrenching sobs of anguish. 'You taught me so much in such a short time, thing's that I'll never forget. And *I will*, one day, avenge your murder, or die in the process.'

Through tears and a mental fog, I looked up when I felt a hand rest on my shoulder.

'My condolences on your loss, son,' said the butcher, 'but surely you knew those two are really bad bastards and he should have taken more care. Nevertheless, you'll have to make arrangements to have the body removed from my shopfront.'

The butcher departed, but not before delivering a final, totally dispassionate demand. 'And make it sooner rather than later if you don't mind. This sort of display ain't good for business.'

I was far too emotionally drained to rise to that insensitive and unnecessary insult. But, as I stood, I quickly realised eight, near naked, very black aboriginal men surrounded me.

I felt no fear when Jimmy stepped forward and said, 'We see everything, but too far for boomerang. My mob now take good care our brother ... so he can return to Dream Time and forever be in peace. Now it time you must go home, but no feel bad; Adam's spirit always be with you.'

To my never-ending gratitude, Jimmy and his men then lifted Adam from the boardwalk and disappeared into the scrub beside the butcher's shop.

20

L eading Adam's horse, I rode back to the camp site, my thoughts and emotions fluttering between disbelief, loneliness, hunger, and fear for my safety, but worst of all, how would I relay to Rocky and my stepfamily, what had just happened.

My spirits were given a nudge upwards as Jack raced up to greet me, his body quivering, tail thumping and offering small yaps of welcome. 'You're a champion Jack, but as you can see, all's not well ... and we'll be returning home empty handed as soon as we've had something to eat.'

I soon got the fire going again. About ten minutes later, we both finally got a half-decent meal; both of us each making short work of a huge Scotch fillet steak and sausages. No time for a cuppa, so I packed Adam's and my saddlebags, then checked the legs of all four horses for any joint hot spots or cracked hooves.

I was about to tether all the horses into a train but remembered how previously they had tagged along without any restraint. So be it, I swung up into my saddle, collected my reins and gently heel-tapped my horse's ribs. Jack also seemed anxious to get going and bounded into the lead, no doubt a fair bet in his mind that he was going home.

The return trail was, in places, equally precipitous and downright scary, but we successfully navigated that terrain without incident. Given most of the trail was downhill, I made good time and arrived at the Wonnangatta Station just before nightfall.

Jack had raced ahead, perhaps anticipating a happy reunion with Jim, but it was sad to see his disappointment. Poor Jack, he must have sensed the hut was unnaturally deserted for he started howling and ran back into the hut as if expecting Jim to be hiding somewhere inside.

I elected not to sleep in the hut that night, but set up camp outside, hopefully where I would remain up-wind of the long-drop.

It was pleasant sitting beside the fire, feeling its heat blunting the chill of the night air and sipping sweetened black tea while sharing my dinner and the Milky Way with Jack. He lay, resting his head upon my leg. This circumstance no doubt confused Jack for he occasionally lifted his head and growled ... as if a familiar noise of the night heralded Jim's return.

At dawn the next morning, I kicked the fire back to life and soon had the billy boiling. None of the horses had strayed far and when I called them, they all made their way back to the hut.

After downing two mugs of heavily sweetened tea, I rolled up my swag, fitted saddles, and bridles, then packed and attached the saddle bags and both swags. Of course, Jack supervised, following me from task to task. After a quick visit to the long drop, I walked to the nearby creek, washed my hands, and splashed several handfuls of water on my face. If I wasn't already wide awake, I was by then.

I walked back to the hut with Jack. With my boots, I spread what remained of the fire's ashes and had a final look around this remote, beautiful location.

Next, I squatted beside Jack and gently held his handsome head so that we were looking directly into each other's face. 'Mate, you're more than welcome to return home with me. It's a bit of a distance, but you can do it.'

Having mounted, I urged my horse forward. As if I had given each of the other horses a direct instruction, they all dutifully followed.

About two hundred yards from the hut as we were about to enter the tree line, Jack stopped. He then ran around in a tight circle, and again, abruptly stopped, and sat. I sensed he was confused, his instinct to remain and wait for Jim Barclay to return, conflicting with an equally strong sense to remain with the hand that had been feeding him.

Loyalty won out. Without further delay, Jack stood, barked once in my direction then loped away. With a heavy heart, I watched him go knowing I'd greatly miss his company.

Nevertheless, when Jack was about halfway back to the hut, he stopped and turned to perhaps check on my progress.

A mournful howl quickly followed: a damn good dog, that Jack.

I raised my right arm and waved farewell.

21

I made particularly good time considering it was somewhat of a taxing return journey in places. But what made it easier all round, was that I also had Adam's horse to ride; it too was a grand, sure-footed mount who seemed to enjoy every challenge I put to it.

When I arrived at Rocky's property late that afternoon, I noticed a small thread of smoke wafting skyward from the chimney of the old house which stood close to the formal entrance gate to Rocky's property. I chose to ride on rather than investigate, after all, I was tired and my backside and thighs ached; plus, it was easy to convince myself it was none of my business.

Of course, I was looking forward to a good night's sleep. However, I must confess, most of my thoughts, for most of that day, had centred upon Fay. Whether healthy or not, occasional warm and lustful thoughts had at least momentarily unburdened me of some of a terrible anguish which had settled on me.

As I descended the track leading to Rocky's homestead, I agonised about how to best explain what had happened to Adam. When about thirty yards from the main house the front door flew open. Fay quickly appeared and took a few steps out onto the veranda, hands on her hips, while rhythmically tapping her foot … the sun's late afternoon rays immediately lighting up her gorgeous face.

Before she took another step, I had thrown myself from the saddle, no longer aware of my aches and pain, and started sprinting toward her; five, ten but not fifteen steps passed when Fay met my charge. We embraced, almost falling, but recovered to kiss; frantically at first, but then settling into a warm, full-on expression of, well yes, love.

Only when we broke that kiss was I aware we had company. Fay and I untangled ourselves and stood, now side-by-side, gawping in embarrassment at our audience.

All round happy smiles and laughter, mingled with a few cheers and soft clapping, followed. Suddenly everyone was trying to hug Fay and me. And questions in quick order were coming from everyone … until Rocky stepped into the melee.

Without a smile, looking squarely into my eyes demanding my total attention, Rocky said, very loudly, 'God dammit, where's Adam!?'

My salvation came in the most unexpected manner. I was about to speak when Paul screamed and went flying. He landed flat on his back with a thump, about a yard from our small gathering, still holding the stick which I immediately suspected he'd used to irritate my horse, who was known to have a short temper.

The kick delivered to Paul had obviously done some damage. I found myself smiling as Max, Elspeth and Bertie ran to him, expecting the worst. However, in that confusion and without a word, Rocky grabbed my arm and led me about twenty yards away, to get out of ear shot of the others I correctly sensed.

'Right, son, what's happened to Adam? It's serious, isn't it? And no bullshit.'

'He's dead; murdered by that traitorous bastard, Bamford.'

'Were you able to stop him, like?'

'No, but I did get one shot at him. Hit his elbow; I couldn't come at shooting him in the back, though I wish I had.

'And Adam, how did he cop it?'

'A fluke shot to his head. I'd say he was dead before he hit the ground. Rocky, I doubt if he suffered.'

'OK, that's enough for now Leon, you can tell me every detail when you get a bit of peace and quiet, but right now, what do we tell the others? And the police?' Well, maybe not the police; we'll decide that later.'

'Let's just tell everyone—cops included—that Adam is staying with his aboriginal brothers. That's the truth, in fact; they carried his body away with them, though God only knows where to. We don't need to tell the others more than that for now. Just act as naturally as possible until we find the right moment.

'You're a good lad Leon and I trust you explicitly, but this news hurts like hell. You go inside and have a cuppa and a chat with the others. You do realise Fay has missed you somewhat? Anyway I've got something to do in Adam's room which can't wai... .'

He turned abruptly and started quickly walking toward the storage shed. But I'd not missed either the catch in his voice or the attempt to brush away tears which had welled in his eyes.

I soon realised Paul was missing and concluded the others had carried him inside for whatever treatment could be administered.

Fay however, had led all the horses into the home paddock and was already in the process of unsaddling one of them. She looked up at me, smiled and with an arm, gesturing that I should leave her to it and go inside.

I blew her a kiss, turned, wandered up to the house then stepped onto the veranda. I casually reached for the front door's doorknob but instinctively stopped, rigid: *boots off first mate!*

An involuntary shudder raised the hairs down the middle of my back. To this very day, I'm still positive I'd just heard Adam's voice as he issued those instructions to me on the day we first set foot on this property.

'He's in his room Leon,' Bertie muttered, genuinely grappling with the emotion of seeing his brother in such a dire condition. 'Mum and Dad are with him. Will he live Leon?'

'Give me a break Bertie, I've only just got home. I hope so, but he should've known better than to antagonise the horses. He should know at his age that all animals feel pain and given the opportunity will lash out to defend themselves.'

* * *

THIS WASN'T the cheerful return I was expecting as I entered Paul's bedroom. Elspeth and Max were seated on opposite sides of their son's bed, each holding one of Paul's lifeless hands. Understandably, both parents wore grief-stricken faces; both had been crying.

Paul didn't move, and I couldn't detect whether he was breathing or not. His face had a waxy, gray pallor which I'd only too recently witnessed: goddamn it, now Bertie too was dead!

Max was first to speak, albeit in a croaky, shaky voice. 'He's gone, Leon. That damn horse of yours kicked our boy so hard it smashed all his ribs ... and killed him!'

'Look, of course I'm deeply saddened too, Max and Elspeth, but we can't blame my horse. Paul was antagonising it when he should have realised it was tired, and no doubt thirsty and hungry. And we've both chastised him previously for doing the exact same thing.'

'Yes, I concede that, but this is a terrible thing to have happened to our family ... and everything happened so damn fast. Elspeth and I will miss our boy dreadfully.'

Unbeknown to me, Rocky had entered the bedroom and said, almost inaudibly, 'As you both should, but not as much as I'll miss Adam.'

22

———————

The mood within the house was one of abject despair. Even after I'd built up the fire into a hearty roar, its heat did little to take the chill out of that gloomy room.

When Fay entered Paul's room about half an hour later, she gracefully went to his bedside, kissed the fingertips of her right hand, then touched them to her brother's forehead. The Christian gesture of a cross which followed sent Elspeth into another understandable outburst of grief.

Max then walked around the bed and swept up his wife and daughter, hugging them firmly. When they moved apart, Fay's eyes were downcast but showed very little emotion. In fact, I don't believe her eyes held any tears whatsoever.

With deliberately strong steps she left her brother's bedside and strode toward the kitchen, catching me by my wrist and almost frog marched me to the kitchen.

Rocky was sitting quietly at the kitchen table, deep in thought I suspect, but looked up immediately at our entrance and said, 'Right, you two, outside.'

Fay glanced at me coquettishly then grabbed my hand and

headed for the front door with me in tow. '*So, what the Hell's going on now?*' I asked myself on this day of unarranged surprises.

Parked directly adjacent to the front steps was a two-seater buggy. 'On you get, one on each side of me,' Rocky ordered, and the buggy soon became a three-seater, albeit a bit squeezy. Before I could protest, Rocky flicked the reins and the horse lurched forward, causing the first laughter I'd heard for some time as Fay, and I scrambled for handholds to stop us from falling.

Rocky remained silent, feigning he was totally absorbed in controlling the buggy, rather than answering my justified questioning.

When we reached the crest of the rise, apparently heading for the gate to Rocky's property, Rocky hauled the buggy to a stop and said proudly while grinning like a loon, 'Well, kids, it's all yours.'

Fay, now also grinning madly, stretched her right arm behind Rocky's back and punched my shoulder, quite hard. 'What do yah reckon my handsome man? It's ours, all ours.'

Still not certain what the two of them were talking about, Rocky came to my rescue. 'The house, Leon, the house and all the land surrounding it is yours ... for as far as you can see on this side of the fence.'

'Good God Almighty,' I replied, and after a few mute seconds to allow reality to sink in, I added, 'definitely not the homecoming I was expecting. But this is an incredibly generous gift, Rocky. Mind you, I've no idea what I've done to deserve this. It's a dream come true; what I've always wanted.'

'Consider it an early marriage gift from me: all the trimmings inside are gifts from Elspeth and Max.'

When the buggy stopped rocking directly outside the front door of the old hut, Rocky gently but firmly restrained us from dismounting and said. 'It's not so much what you two have done, but rather, what you'll achieve with your lives.

'Look, I can't hang about; I've got matters to attend to in Wangaratta. Somebody must explain to the police what's befallen our family, and I'll need to organise a burial service for Bertie. Time permitting, I'll plant a few ideas into the minds of the senior copper so that some justice might be extracted for Adam. Now, go on, get back inside.

'I'll stay overnight in Wang, so, see you tomorrow sometime.' With that said he flicked the reins, and the buggy shot forward.

23

Once inside, Fay grabbed my hand. 'C'mon, let me show you around.'

I resisted slightly, in so much that I wanted to learn if I could see the front gate from the kitchen and hopefully get a parting glimpse of Rocky ... which I did.

Rocky had just shut the properties front gate and was about to climb back aboard the buggy to resume his visit to Wangaratta, when he turned and waved.

What he'd missed in the meantime, were our antics when Fay had insisted that I should carry her through the front door of our own home.

Fay then took total control. 'This way Leon,' she said, again taking hold of my hand. Although the grand tour was brief, it was clear to me that a fair amount of work had recently gone into preparing the old hut to make it clean and comfortable.

'Mum and Dad and me and my brothers nearly broke our backs giving this place a new life. We did it while you were away with Adam. And all that stuff in the kitchen was purchased by Mum and Dad, in Wang. We got rid of heaps of spider's webs and dust and dirt from the floors and scrubbed like mad. Dad checked the plumbing and the boys, I must say, actually did a good job of helping Dad'.

'And everything smells so nice and clean.' I added in my best complimentary tone of voice, but quickly asked most pragmatically. 'Did Max also check the condition of the roof?'

'Oh yes, of course. And I just knew you'd ask me that; he not only repaired the entire roof, but he had to straighten the chimney and re-cement the bricks.

'Now, Leon, let me show you our bedroom, where all the really hard work took place.'

As Fay dragged me into the bedroom, I was astounded. Not only was there a huge, wooden framed double bed overflowing with blankets and a heap of pillows, but a brand new, highly polished matching redwood wardrobe, and a fashionable green coloured carpet covered the entire floor. A small, glazed window was positioned above the bedhead, and someone, probably Elspeth, had fitted bright green curtains around its frame.

Up against the opposite wall was a small wooden table, its top covered with a white lace doily. An earthenware water jug and a matching, large diameter bowl and an oil lantern sat neatly on the table. Hanging from nails protruding from the wall on either side of the table were matching towels.

As my observations concluded, the fragrance of Fay's hair and the clean scent of her body had not gone unnoticed; in fact, a tingling in my gentleman's region, shortness of breath and a sudden dryness in my mouth conspired to have me sneak up behind her, wrap my arms around her waist and impulsively cup my hands over her surprisingly large and firm breasts.

In a husky, sensual voice feigning shock, Fay said, challengingly, 'Oh my, you cheeky boy. This is very forward of you Leon; just as well your intentions are honourable.'

* * *

OFFERING VERY LITTLE RESISTANCE, I was dragged onto that magnificent bed. Fay was desperately trying to undo the belt of my trousers, yet I saw no reason why I shouldn't assist her efforts. Our shoes hit the floor with a clatter and my trousers followed seconds later. Somehow Fay had released the clasp holding the back of her skirt together and was now wriggling feverishly to remove her arms and her torso ... to successfully expose her beautiful, magnificent breasts. She brushed aside my groping hands and commenced fumbling with the buttons on my shirt, but clearly the poor girl needed my help. I swung my legs over the side of the bed, and no sooner had I removed and discarded my shirt, and now completely naked, turned to face Fay.

Having no idea how gorgeous the naked female body could be, I stared at the stunning young woman before me on the opposite side of the bed. Our eyes locked. I think my breathing stopped. I was aware my mouth was dry, and I could feel my heart beating, rapidly. Light-headedness forced me to take a few deep breaths. And, I was now very aware of an intense excitement and anticipation, much more powerful than the previous, albeit pleasant tingling in my gentleman's region.

Fay looked stunned as she gazed at my offering ... a very erect, pulsating display of my manhood.

As if reading each-other's minds, we leapt in unison onto the bed, launched into a passionate embrace, kissed, then collapsed entwined onto the bed; our first naked intimacy.

More kissing, frenzied fondling, neck nibbling and fumbling quickly followed. Impatience gave way to success when Fay very subtly surrendered to allow me full penetration. In a mutual wave of sensual bliss, we collapsed, yet still partially entwined, side-by-side onto the bed; our respective virginity, now lost. (I did wonder the next day, how Fay knew about the art of oral sex, mind blowing as it was.)

I doubt that Fay was reading my thoughts, but suddenly we stared at each other. I had no idea what triggered it, but our smiles turned to us laughing like loons on top note. A gentle wrestling match of sorts followed, before we again returned to a side-by-side position.

Our near state of exhaustion soon returned to something like normal, at which time Fay quietly asked, 'Darling, what really happened to Adam?'

Not what I expected, but she had a right to know. We squiggled beneath the blankets and about an hour later, everything I knew and felt about the murderer, and of Adam's death, had been revealed to her.

Now, feeling overwhelmingly comfortable and spent, we both fell into a deep sleep. I think I must have snored because I recall getting an elbow jabbed into my ribs on a few occasions.

* * *

Two months of domestic bliss followed. And in hindsight, I had fun with Fay, helping with housework and constructing a fenced garden patch in which we planted vegetables, two cherry trees, a quince tree, and built two parallel mounds of strawberries. Water and shade were plentiful in our chosen location, and fertiliser was, well, plentiful and always nearby.

I also encouraged Fay to try her hand at fishing, and under my expert tutelage she not only soon became very proficient but loved collecting bait. It wasn't long before her catch rate exceeded mine. She also loved exploring the Buckland River searching for water holes where we caught more, and larger trout.

Other than on weekends, each morning I'd wander over to the homestead to help Rocky with any jobs he wanted done.

Max, too, was always happy to work with us. He took great care of the horses and kept an eye on the dozen cattle which roamed Rocky's leasehold. But mostly, I think, he loved working with Rocky when it came to repairing or replacing saddles, reins and ropes.

And, surprise, surprise, Bertie even started showing some interest in "working the farm", but his major contribution was in the kitchen; he loved baking bread with Elspeth and Fay and deserved the accolades we heaped upon him. Bertie also excelled in the art of making ginger beer.

However, the greatest surprise came out of the blue. 'So, Dad, when do I go to boarding school?' Bertie asked in a manner that sounded more like "when" rather than "can I?"

'How about you and I head into Wang tomorrow and ask a few questions. In the meantime, I'll have a talk with Rocky. He'll no doubt know the right person to ask.'

And indeed, he did; in fact, unbeknown to both Max and Bertie, Bertie would soon be following in Adam's scholastic footsteps.

Bertie flourished. He adored life at boarding school and the academic challenges which confronted him. What none of us knew of course was that his home visits would become fewer and fewer, and shorter, and that just two years later, after winning a scholarship which took him to Melbourne, he just, well, disappeared!

However, some salacious rumours reached us suggesting Bertie was heavily involved in brewing beer, somewhere in Central Western Victoria. But that's entirely another story.

24

────────

About mid-morning, the day after, Max and Bertie went into Wangaratta to sort out "Berties call to boarding school".

While Fay and I were tidying up after breakfast, we heard the unmistakeable, rhythmic sounds of an approaching horses' hoof beats. 'Visitors' darling,' Fay said brightly. 'Well, come on, let's go see who it is.'

Not surprisingly it was Rocky; but it was, however, a total surprise to see Jimmie (Adam's mob brother) sitting beside him in the buggy.

'Well, g'day you two, looks like you've settled in nicely, I must say?' Rocky said with a wink while nodding in our direction where we stood with our arms around each other's waist.

'Well, well Jimmie, nice that we meet again,' I said happily while trotting around to his side of the buggy. We shook hands. I was about to introduce him to Fay, but she almost pushed me over in her excitement to meet him and introduce herself. 'Thank you, Jimmie, for saving Leon from being killed.'

A bemused Jimmie shook the hand Fay offered, and smiling broadly he said quietly, 'Nice ta know yah, missus. This 'ere fella yours, he good man; my bruddah.'

'Jimmie's got some news for you Leon,' said Rocky, but how about a cuppa first?'

Fay was off like a shot back into the kitchen. I wondered later if she knew we were about to have visitors.

'I say, Rocky, will Jimmie feel intimidated being in our house ... and talking openly with us in front of Fay?' I asked.

'Dat no prob, Leon,' Jimmie answered for himself.

When we entered the kitchen, Fay ushered us to sit at the kitchen table. Jimmie seemed at ease, gazing around the room, nodding to himself now and then as if giving his personal approval.

As I passed around mugs and side plates, Fay followed me pouring each of us a steaming hot brew of black tea. Rocky pushed the sugar bowl into the space in front of Jimmie. Fay produced plates of biscuits and sultana filled scones and then sat between me and Jimmie.

'Welcome Jimmie, you're our very first visitor to our house,' said Fay. 'Please, you help yourself.'

Jimmie didn't need further encouragement, ladling four heaped teaspoons of sugar into his tea while reaching for a scone. More nodding of approval followed when he bit into his scone and then sipped his tea, 'Mmmm, much more betta than my woman she makes.' he said.

A minute or so lapsed before Rocky spoke. 'Strange thing happened when I was in Wang. I had the feeling Jimmie, and his mob were looking for me. It's happened before, quite often actually, when Adam was with me. Anyway, when I was a couple of miles out of Wang, there was Jimmie and his mob on the side of the road waiting for me. Couldn't believe it at first, but I pulled over and we had quite a chin wag.'

'Jimmie, you ready to now tell Leon and Fay what you told me?'

'OK, now is good time. That fella Bamford who kill Adam, we find him and point bone at him. He now getting sick every day. Hair fallin' out and loosin' his teeth. Our kurdaitcha spirit man, he pays him many visits. Dat fella's time soon be up. But he don't know it yet.'

'That's really interesting Jimmie, but how *did* you find him? I asked, genuinely interested.

'He not able fix his elbow after you shoot him. He be askin''round for help from our clever man, or white man doctor. We do not help him, and he should know no doctors in high country. Was easy tah find him, he always drunk. Made it easy for kurdaitcha man to approach to point bone and sing his death time song. No footprints left by our kurdaitcha man; maybe find few feathers, but no footprints.'

'For the benefit of Fay and Leon,' said Rocky. '*The clever man*, or *kurdaitcha man* is like a witch doctor, a chosen elder blessed with supernatural powers, including *the act of pointing the bone* to hasten the death of someone who has done the wrong thing by their mob.

'The closer the *clever man* gets to his target; the stronger will be the suffering inflicted. Mind games actually. The target convinces himself he can see the kurdaitcha man in his dreams, like a devil coming to kill him. The more the target thinks about what's going on in his head, the worse things get for him, like an unshakeable merry-go-round of images. The target apparently becomes so absorbed and fearful of dying that he induces his very own lethal heart attack.

'Oh yes, I nearly forgot; the feathers which Jimmie referred to are real enough. To get close to his target, the clever man wraps both of his feet in emu feathers to muffle the sound of his foot falls and to ensure he leaves no human footprints.'

'But that's not all, eh Jimmie?' Rocky asked purposefully. 'Please, tell Leon and Fay what else you know.'

'Dat other white fella, the one I hit so well with ma best kylie, he gone north ... not help Bamfud, just up and gone. On his own, with one of mister Barclay's best horses.'

'But Jimmie, why are you so sure it was that fella, Mickey?' I asked politely.

'Two brothers my mob an' me, we know that white fella. Bad bugga that one. He always tryin' tah pick fight with us. Stole our money to buy grog.'

'And where do you believe he's headed up north?' Fay asked persuasively, realising Jimmie had not yet told us everything.

'We hear him one time screamin' at Bamfud 'bout bein' lazy and that if he didn't get arm fixed, he'd take off on his own to a place called Dorrigo, where it much more easy to take cattle than here. And no police.

'You go after Bamfud first, Rocky, he not get far in his condition. Then I show you which way to Dorrigo to find Mickey?'

Before Rocky could reply, out of the blue came the least expected response imaginable. In a firm, determined voice while looking straight into my eyes, Fay said, 'When can we be ready to leave darling.'

'In two days,' Rocky interrupted, 'I'll not miss this chase, no matter how bad me bloody legs are.

'Jimmie, you and your mob can stay with me until we're ready to leave. There's all you'll need in the shed furthest from the house.'

'Only me here, this time Rocky.'

'OK then, Jimmie, you can use Adam's rooms in the shed if you wish.

'God dammit, I vow I *will* find those two and bring them both to justice,' Rocky added sternly, 'either dead, or alive: over my dead body if necessary!'

25

It was only fair now, that Elspeth and Max be advised of our intentions. Addressing them, after outlining our plans, Rocky said, 'There's no changing our minds, we *are* going ahead with this.

'So, I'd be eternally grateful if you two would manage the homestead and keep an eye on things while we're gone. I can't tell you how long we'll be away; it could be only a few days, or it could be weeks. It depends upon how quickly we can locate Bamford. Don't worry you two. Leon, Jimmie and his mob, and me, will take care of Fay.

'As far as Mickey's concerned, he's got a few weeks head start on us, so, whether we can get after him straight away will be up to Jimmie's mob.'

'I've got a question for you, Jimmie,' Elspeth asked. 'Do you know where Adam is buried?'

'Oh yes, missus,' Jimmie replied. 'In sacred place in high country … his family country. My mob, we've done long-time cleansing ceremony to help loved ones with their loss, and same time send his spirit onto next part his journey.

'We go first dat sacred place, then consider how we deal with dat Bamfud fella. Next, we see if dat Mickey fella leaves us any signs.'

* * *

THE FOLLOWING day was devoted to selecting our horses, checking their general health and ensuring their shoes were fitting correctly, and secure. Six horses were chosen; all would be rotated as either mounts or as pack horses. All were walers; tried, true and trusted for their mountain work, at which they excelled.

After our evening's dinner, in that period approaching twilight when the flies retire and the mosquitoes emerge hungry for your blood, we all spent an hour or so checking saddles and associated leather items. Most items were suitably sound, yet Max stayed on alone in the main shed making good any items which needed repair or replacement. He only returned to the house after his lantern ran out of fuel. A good bloke, my stepfather.

The next morning, we methodically packed clothing, spare boots, rolled our swags, checked our sidearms and packed plenty of ammunition, just in case.

Fay was initially put-out that Rocky refused to supply her with a gun. She was suitably appeased when Rocky said with genuine passion, 'in the event of a shoot-out, or an ambush, we need someone capable of ensuring we all have plenty of ammo readily to hand. There's no one here better able to do that job than you.'

'Yeah, OK. But I still want to learn how to shoot straight with one of those six shooters.'

Jimmie loathed guns: but he had total trust in his skills with his long throwing sticks, and faithful kylie. And he could ride really well as we soon discovered. 'Adam taught him well,' Rocky told us with pride.

That afternoon we finished packing essential provisions; flour, salt and sultanas for making damper, tea, sugar, cheeses, smoked chicken, sausage and home-made barley sugar, mugs, plus pots and a variety of cooking utensils ... and toilet paper.

After dinner, content that our loading time would be minimal in the cold of tomorrow's early morning, we all retired just as the moon rose over mount Murray's rugged peak, the signal for resident mopokes to commence calling to any nearby, potential mates.

* * *

ELSPETH, Max and Fay prepared an enjoyable breakfast of lightly smoked bacon, home-made beef sausages, eggs, fried onions and tomatoes, followed by toast and plum jam. There was no shortage of tea, however the usual need for seconds was declined, overcome by the urge to get underway.

The morning had dawned cool but filled with anticipation; the horses were already in the home yard and were at the side fence eyeing off our every move.

Having saddled and fitted bridles to our selected mounts, we then shared with loading the packhorses. Halters were fitted to the pack-horses though we all knew they were unlikely to see much use; they could be relied upon to follow.

'Ah, that's what I've been looking for,' Rocky announced with a grin. 'The last buckle that needs tightening. C'mon, let's get going, shall we?'

<h1 style="text-align:center">26</h1>

About five miles from the settlement of Porepunkah, now below Mount Buffalo which towered above us, Jimmie, who'd been leading our party, suddenly reined in his horse. As we gathered around, Jimmie said confidently, 'Two horses they come dis same way. Not so long ago, an' not far ahead, I reckon. They have fire; maybe they give us nice cuppa. But maybe not. You see there? Horses shod; my guess those two be coppers.'

'Well spotted,' replied Rocky, 'but just in case, Leon, you know the drill... '

'Yeah, I know ... put one up the spout, just in case, like.'

'C'mon, keep moving,' said Rocky, confident and unflustered. 'I'll do all the talking, OK'.

The track ahead led directly to a well-used crossing point of the Buckland River, a location where I'd crossed on four previous occasions. On the elevated bank on the far side of the river where Adam and I had once camped overnight, two men stood observing our approach, both cradling rifles and both unmistakably police. Strange how a blue uniform jacket could convey such immediate authority.

Rocky reined in his horse, signalling the rest of us to do likewise.

'Been waiting long Senior Carmichael?' Rocky called across the river. 'Don't suppose you've got the billy on for a cuppa?'

'Always got time for a man of his word,' the senior replied, his voice clear above the gentle babbling of the river. 'Come on over, you lot. We need to talk.'

Having crossed the clear cold river without incident, we all dismounted. Jimmie and Fay immediately took charge of the horses, ushering them back to the river's edge to drink. Rocky strode confidently up to face Mr. Carmichael, with me in tow following closely. They shook hands.

'G'day Don,' said Rocky. 'Thanks for agreeing to meet here. This is my nephew, Leon Rosser, the lad I was telling you about. Not long out from England with his family and now my apprentice stud master, and invaluable roustabout.'

'Nice to meet you Leon,' said Mr. Carmichael, as we in turn shook hands. 'But pray tell, who are the other two over there, I need to meet them; call them over if you would Leon.'

'The lady is my wife, Fay,' I replied proudly, 'and the other chap is Jimmie, a close friend and our tracker.'

Don's eyebrows had shot up sharply at these revelations. 'My assistant is private Cameron, first name Daniel, though he prefers to be called Dan. He's been posted to me, all the way from Warrnambool. A likeable lad, good with horses and he's not a bad tracker as well. He should get on well with your man, Jimmie.

'See to it that they get introduced straight away, please Leon. Then we'll all get comfortable around the fire for a cuppa and a friendly chin wag.'

The fire was quickly booted up into something serviceable. Two billies of gin clear river water were soon boiling, then handfuls of tea were dropped into each billy. Mugs of various shape and vintage appeared as if by magic.

Rocky and I each carefully retrieved a billy from the fire and expertly (I reckon) completed the windmilling process that would ensure the best brew. We then walked around the gathering, filling each person's mug as we went.

Conversation was initially subdued. Sensing some awkwardness, I retrieved some of our homemade barley sugar from my saddle bags, broke it into generous pieces, then placed them onto a dinner plate.

'Here, Dan, get some of this inta yah,' I said jovially, 'then pass on the plate.'

Dan returned my smile, but to my surprise, he stood, walked over to Fay and handed her the plate. 'Ladies first, eh'.

'Best damn barley sugar I think I've ever tasted,' said the Senior, while licking his lips.

'Why, thank you Don,' Fay replied, 'but time's slipping by, and you said we needed to talk.'

'Right you are, Fay,' Don replied, refraining from further unnecessary comment.

'Nevertheless, before we get into the nitty-gritty, you all need to know that Rocky and I have been good friends for many years, and we've resolved a few unsociable and potentially dangerous situations over the years; matters which I couldn't have sorted without his help. And we're here today because of what Rocky conveyed to me a few days ago.

'It would seem there's been some unrest and murders up on the high country, not to mention significant duffing. I'm aware now of Adam's and Jim Barclay's murders and I won't tolerate that sort of going's on in my patch.

'But in this case, I'm not the spring chicken I once was—nor are you Rocky my friend — so, I'm going to allow your intervention on my behalf. A bit unorthodox, but you all have a greater motivation to put a stop to the activities of those few ruthless and nasty bastards.

'You all seem well enough equipped and if Rocky has chosen you to support him, you'll be in good hands. I'll overlook the fact that Rocky and Leon have side arms, but what about you Fay, do I have to give you permission to also carry arms?'

Rocky quickly spoke up. 'The girl needs a bit more practice with a six shooter, but she's a pretty good shot with her rifle. We could do with a bit more ammo if you can spare some Don.'

'Good, I feel a bit better knowing that, I think,' Don replied, but quickly added, 'I'd like to empower all of you, including Jimmie, to be "constables assisting"... but only until you return, whenever that might be. Regardless, I can't give you the go-ahead; not until I'm happy with your answers to a few questions.'

'Hang on a second Don,' Rocky interrupted. 'Do I understand it from your words, that you won't be joining us?'

'Correct, not this time mate. I'm getting too damn old for this caper. However, how would you feel about having Daniel, I mean, Dan, tag along? Besides, someone needs to be manning the station in Wang, just in case I need to vouch for your undertakings.'

'So, Dan, how do you feel about joining Rocky's team? You've got a good horse under you, and you've got plenty of provisions ... and you could benefit from the experience. Remembering that Rocky will be calling the shot's; no pun intended.'

'Happy to, boss,' Dan replied with a cheeky smile. 'But you're a slippery one, senior. I was wonderin' why you wanted me to bring along me sleepin' bag —an' you didn't—and the packhorse... now I get it. But I aren't agree'n to nuthin'... not until I've heard Rocky's answers to your questions.'

'Cheeky bugger. Most of what I packed into your saddle bags are body bags. See to it young man that your new team doesn't need any of them for you.

'Right then; Rocky, why is it that Leon hasn't joined the Australian Army?'

'Fair enough question,' Rocky answered quickly, 'but we both know he's exempt because he's a valued primary producer.'

'And how will you instruct your team to act if they come under direct fire. I'm aware there are other bad bastards still roaming the high country; the type who might instigate a surprise and deadly shootout, hoping to steal your horses for example, or worse, to kidnap Fay.'

'Don, you can rely upon me to encourage my team to do whatever's necessary to protect each other and our property ... but with just sufficient force of course.'

'Yeah, right ... what you really mean is that you'll shoot first to kill and answer any questions later. Right?'

'We've always understood each other, eh Don?'

'What about you, Dan?' Rocky asked. 'Do you still now want in with us?'

'Yeah boss,' Dan replied, 'at least one of us has to look the part, an' I have no gut bustin' need to bugger up our Don and Dan show.'

'Cheeky bastard,' Don chuckled. 'What say you, Jimmie? Can you work with private Cameron?'

'Thought you never ask,' Jimmie replied matter-of-factly, 'he quick learner I reckon, but will probably need much more ammo than all of us. An' if Dan needed, he can run a lot more quicker than Rocky can, I reckon.'

* * *

It only took a few minutes to repack our saddle bags, and to extinguish our fire.

'If I get a move on, I should be back in Wang before it gets dark,' Don commented as he swung up into his saddle. 'Go carefully, old friend, but do what you must Rocky; I vow there will be no consequences.'

They shook hands. 'I must say, Rocky, young Leon and Fay make a great couple; he'd make a decent copper given the chance.'

'I don't reckon that's his go, Don. He's been dreaming of owning his own property and I can't see Fay scrubbing out cell floors in a police station.'

'Maybe, but he's mature for his age and I sense both Jimmie and private Cameron already respect him.

'Anyway, thanks again Rocky for taking on this manhunt.

'Good luck you lot,' Don called to us, saluted, then turned his horse toward the river. Suddenly he reined in his horse, swivelled in his saddle and yelled, 'Make sure you spend some time with that butcher in Grant; my gut feeling tells me he knows a lot more than he's willingly prepared to disclose.'

The rest of us then saddled up and headed in single file onto the track leading to the Wonnangatta Station. Once again, huge eucalyptus trees towered above us, their canopies whispering overhead.

A flock of ten or so cockatoos suddenly launched into flight, screeching their indignance at our passage, shattering the peace and harmony I was feeling, and I daresay, the contentment or anticipation the others were likely to have been experiencing. Such was the surprise that Dan's horse started pigrooting, failing badly to send Dan somewhere to sit other than in his saddle.

I looked back, intending to give a final departure wave to Senior Carmichael, but alas, he had already forded the river and was out of sight.

Only then did I start thinking about a very special friend ... a four legged one.

27

———

Now being familiar with the terrain and the track's obstacles, I felt confident leading our party at a good clip. Our horses responded magnificently with sure-footed grace, and we arrived at the lower reaches of a large clearing which heralded our arrival at the Wonnangatta Station with still at least an hour of daylight remaining ... but sadly no welcoming bark from Jack. [*I learnt, years later, that Jack was found in a terrible state of neglect by a neighbouring farmer who took ownership of him. However, Jack died from wounds inflicted during a fight with a resident male dingo.*]

The Station hut, to our surprise, was locked. No doubt we could have easily broken in, but Dan informed us that the hut was now a crime scene. 'Mind you, if it were rainin' or blowin' a gale, or snowin' for that matter, it'd be entirely different. But it ain't, so we'll be under the stars tonight.'

As the sun sank below the horizon, the temperature dropped rapidly. The horses were quickly liberated from their loads, led to the creek for a well-earned drink, then ushered into the home paddock. Fay and I first brushed their backs free of any dust or grit, then curry combed each in turn. Medium weight horse rugs were then fitted without fuss, a necessity rather than a luxury, for the night temperatures at our present altitude can get close to freezing.

Dan, Jimmie and Rocky had collected a small mountain of firewood, and flames were already flickering brightly and clawing their way skyward. What little smoke was produced, showed the direction of a lazy breeze which now swept over the clearing.

By the light cast by our fire, we positioned our sleeping bags to avoid any smoke, then set about preparing our evening meal, a relatively meagre affair of beef sausages, bread, biscuits, multiple cups of sweetened black tea and a piece of barley sugar.

The fire also needed feeding, each time sending another burst of sparks skyward against a black background. However, it was surprising how quickly our wood supply diminished. Fatigue had set in, but we waited to follow the moon slowly elevate itself above the top of the ranges.

Fay and I were the first to retire to our sleeping bags, wanting to be warm and comfortable before the fire gave up its grip on life.

'Good night darling,' Fay whispered. 'Lucky there's no bed bugs to delight.' No more than a minute later, Fay's steady breathing told me she was asleep.

In the light cast by the moon, and even though her blankets covered most of her face, I reflected on how lucky I was; no longer a boy but now a man blessed with the most beautiful wife to be.

I recall rolling onto my back and looking up at the magnificent Milky-Way blazing across the sky. Beautiful yes; but not nearly as lovely as Fay.

The last thing I remember of that day were nearby dingoes presumably howling at the moon.

28

No doubt the call of nature, and the desire to luxuriate in the warmth of a good fire had obviously inspired Rocky, Jimmie and Dan to leave their sleeping bags. Not only was our fire now roaring, but they were sitting side-by-side next to it, chatting quietly and presumably enjoying their first cuppa of the day.

It couldn't have been much fun for Fay, in her modesty, trying to dress within the confines of her bag. But she never complained, just laughed when she realised in her haste that both of her legs would not fit into one trouser leg.

'I suppose you're going to tell me you've already done a day's work,' I jested as Fay and I approached the fire.

'On any normal day that'd be the case,' Rocky replied, leaving me wondering if he was chiding us, or pulling our legs. 'Mind you, we've been making a few decisions. Grab yourselves a brew and I'll fill you in.'

Dan couldn't help himself, reminding us in his own way what he thought of our sleep-in. 'Yah knows what? If you'd stayed in them sleepin' bags any longer, the sun wouldah burnt yah bloody eyes out.' For which he received what appeared to be a quite firm, yet playful punch to his left shoulder from Fay.

'Apparently, according to Jimmie anyway,' Rocky suddenly said, 'we are no more than an hour from where Adam's interred, so, as soon as we've had some breakfast, I intend to pay that place a visit.

'You're all welcome to come with me, of course. However, it's a sacred place and Jimmie must first approach it alone to seek permission from his Dreamtime spirits for all of us to call on Adam. If Jimmie comes back with a *no*, then we must accept their custom and leave that place, and perhaps return another day.'

'Doubt any problem that way, Rocky,' said Jimmie. 'Not evil bone in any of youse bodies. Good thing youse all related to Adam in yah own ways... even if yah don't know it.'

'Cept for me,' replied Dan. 'I'm a good bloke too, but not relative of your man Adam. No disrespect meant; I wish I had known him.

'It's easier for Jimmie if I don't go with you. If it's OK with you Rocky, I'll head for Grant and meet the local mob. Hope they're friendly and can give me a run down on them two blokes we're after.'

'I think you'll be OK Dan,' Rocky replied. 'Mention my name, and Leon ... and that we're here on men's business regarding Adam. Yeah, that should do it.'

With that said, we each went about packing, loading our pack-horses and saddling up. After a visit to the surrounding scrub to satisfy the call of nature—conveniently to the long drop in Fay's case —we all mounted our horses and rode to the northern most end of the Wonnangatta's cleared land.

'Take care Dan,' Rocky called as Dan peeled away from the rest of our party and headed in the direction taken by the cattle stolen by Bamford and Mickey. 'And just in case son, keep one up the spout, eh.'

Dan waved, smiled and called back, 'I'm a step ahead of you this morning Rocky. And, hey Jimmie, I'll call you when I get to Grant.'

'And how the hell's he going to do that?' Fay asked politely of Rocky.

'I'll get Jimmie to explain later, my dear.'

* * *

SADLY, there was still no sign of Jim Barclay's wonderful dog.

29

———————

After an hour of reasonably hard riding, Jimmie called a halt. Apparently, we had reached our destination. Jimmie quickly dismounted and jogged into the thick surrounding scrub. Wherever he'd gone, we could faintly hear his guttural singing voice.

Barely five minutes lapsed before he returned to us, though I don't recall how he did that without spooking the horses, or without anyone of us catching a glimpse of him moving through the undergrowth.

That was strange enough, but after tethering our horses Jimmie led us along a small track which scouted the base of a steep, debris littered cliff face: a track and a cliff face which only minutes before didn't exist. More amazing however, was that given the cliff's incredible height, why was it that none of us, particularly Rocky, had never seen this place beforehand?

An opening in that cliff face appeared. In single file, we dutifully followed Jimmie when he beckoned us to follow him into a cave. I have no recall of being in danger, nor was I surprised when Jimmie led us up an incline, followed then by a sudden descent into a chamber the size of a small shed. Light flooded that chamber though it was impossible to see any openings to the outside world, yet there was a pervading, pleasant scent which I soon discovered came from branches of flowering eucalypt trees, all recently picked, I was certain.

The most unexpected experience of all was that I can't remember talking to anyone, yet I was clearly receiving answers from Jimmie in response to my questions.

Jimmie pointed to a ledge at head height. 'Adam, his body lay here, but spirit long gone to next life in our Dreamtime.' A bundle of kangaroo and possum pelts prevented me from seeing Adam's interred body.

Jimmie's voice continued. 'Our mob very proud of Adam, but you must ask Rocky why.'

I recall shortly after being ushered by Jimmie, albeit without Rocky, first back to the entrance of the cave, and then to where we'd left our horses.

'You now sit here an' wait awhile.' Jimmie's voice instructed Fay and I. 'Rocky has much for me to pass onto Adam; only I can do that.'

'But not to worry, Rocky he joins you soon.'

Only then did I feel the sun on my face, hear birds calling and the tree canopies being rustled overhead by a warming breeze.

'What in heavens name just happened to us darling?' said Fay, speaking my exact same thoughts.

'If I knew that, and how, I'd bottle it if I could. But no harm done; are you OK?'

'Yes, I'm fine,' Fay replied, just a little sleepily. 'I feel relaxed, and you know, sort of honoured. And I never once felt out of place or in any danger whatsoever.

'Oh, look. Here comes Rocky and Jimmie.'

Everything about them appeared normal as they strolled towards us, as if nothing astonishing had just transpired.

'I think Adam will understand your feelings,' Jimmie said quietly. 'An our mob thank you for respecting him, and our customs. But come on, let's get moving. Dan, he lettin' me know he's already in Grant.'

'How the hell could he know that?' asked Fay, loud enough for all of us to hear.

'Ancient trick always in every black man's head,' Jimmie responded with a toothy smile. 'Too hard to teach white fellas. Missus, yes, maybe later…'

'Yeah, right; thanks Jimmie, we'll remember that', Rocky replied, just a wee bit sarcastically. 'However, before we make a move, I want you two to know that in accordance with aboriginal custom, many of Adam's prized belongings were interred with him, including the watch I gave him for his twenty first birthday. Here, Leon it's now yours. I'm sure Adam would have wanted you to have it.'

To this very day I still wear Adam's watch with great pride.

'There's something else he left for you Fay. It's a written confession of sorts. Here, you'd best read it. My advice, if you want it, is that we all need to know what was playing badly on Adam's conscience. It's something we all need to be aware of, but never worry about.'

Fay quickly read the note then handed it to me.

Leon and Fay.

I want you both to know it wasn't entirely your brother Paul's fault that my horse kicked out when it did. I must bear some blame, for it was me who directed that horse to lash out and frighten him; to stop his silly mischief making and tormenting our animals … not to kill him. Adam.

'I'll show this note, and my lovely new watch of course, to Elspeth and Max as soon as we return home,' I said. 'But do yah know what? I for one have never felt that Elspeth was comfortable in Adam's company, but she needs to see the decent sort of bloke he was.

'I realise nothing will bring back Paul, so, I'll let them decide whether to accept Adam's frustration and apology for the grief he unintentionally triggered.

'C'mon, let's get moving. If we hunt the horses along a bit, we might make it into Grant before dark.'

As we swung our horses back to where we separated with Dan at the northern end of the Wonnangatta station, Rocky suddenly called out, 'I wonder who owns that big dog up ahead?'

'Not dog, Rocky,' Jimmie replied, 'that be dingo.'

'But it's black and white,' Fay impatiently objected. 'Every dingo I've ever seen has been a sandy colour. Though, I admit it's got the same build as a dingo.'

'That be Adam's totem animal,' Jimmie explained. 'You're mostly right missus, but believe me, dingoes they can be all white, or black, or a mixup of evry colour.

'This one here maybe even Adam in his new life. If it is, he might tag along, but mostly out of sight. My guess be he'll not do us harm.'

Sadly, it wasn't Jack, though his image was still in my mind.

30

Our horses, even at altitude, moved gracefully and tirelessly. By noon it was apparent we were close to Grant; the normally crystal-clear mountain air was now tainted by the unmistakeable smell of humanity.

'Dan, he be just ahead,' Jimmie called to us, 'round next bend, you'll see.'

True to his word, standing in the middle of the track was Dan.

Fay leant from her saddle and grabbed my arm. 'Again, darling, how could he have known that?'

'Buggered if I know,' I replied, shrugging my shoulders, 'but we'll no doubt find out one of these days.'

'This way, my friends,' said Dan with a flourish of his arm and a welcoming smile.

Dan led us about a hundred yards into the bush to a partly over-grown clearing beside a swift flowing, gin clear creek. As we set about unpacking and freeing our horses of their burdens, a fire was on the make in no time and two billies were in place.

The horses all drank deeply then each received the full grooming treatment though they were perhaps a bit impatient for us to be finished as they had discovered ample pickings surrounding us.

* * *

A FEW HOURS later after a light meal, multiple mugs of sweetened black tea, a welcome two-hour nap and essential private visits well away from our camp site, Rocky finally raised our agenda.

'So, Dan, tell us what you've learnt.'

'Thought you'd never ask,' Dan replied patiently as he threw a few pieces of timber onto the fire. 'You were right Rocky; the local mob were easy to locate and most co-operative.

'In a nutshell, they know where to locate Bamford, but have no idea where Mickey is.

'Bamford's been given the treatment, and I mean ... the real treatment! He's in a terrible state of anxiety since being boned by the kurdaitcha man; actually, touched by the magic bone more than once.

'He walked away from Grant about a week ago and somehow, he's survived the weather and continues to throw fits of madness. Plus, he's starving, so he's not going anywhere.'

'Oh yes he is,' said Rocky with lethal purpose. 'We've still got a few hours of daylight left, so I'll get you to take me to meet that bastard. How far do we need to travel?'

'Ready when you are Rocky. We can be there in about an hour.'

'Right, you can tell me what else you know about Mickey as we go,' Rocky replied. 'But we've got a small problem. I can't leave Fay here on her own, which means, Leon, you'll need to stay with her.'

'Be damned if I'll miss out on this, Rocky,' Fay replied with some anger.

'And neither will I, so that's settled,' I let it be known firmly enough.

Rocky looked a bit piqued, frowning, hands on hips, his mouth opening and closing, but finally he relaxed and added calmly, 'Look, Fay, what's likely to happen when we meet Bamford is not what I want to expose you to. The proceedings will definitely not be memorable.'

'Rocky, I really do appreciate your concerns,' said Fay, placing her hand on Rocky's arm, 'but I've made my decision, so let's get a move on.'

'All right, fair enough,' Rocky replied, 'but that now means our pack horses will remain hobbled here, and that's not such a good idea.'

'Leave it to me Rocky,' Jimmie quickly responded. 'I'll get my mob to keep an eye on things.'

* * *

JIMMIE AND DAN led us towards Mount Howitt, to a location where a decent drop off sloped downward from the ridge line we'd been traversing.

'This be where Bamfud go arse overhead,' advised Jimmie. 'Him roll down here. I go down first with Dan, then you follow when we wave.'

Without hesitation Jimmie and Dan urged their mounts down that slope, both horses on two occasions sliding on their backsides. It looked easy enough, but I'd ridden down similar inclines previously with Adam, and I had no doubt about our walers being able to do it again.

To my surprise, Fay, our least experienced rider, unhesitatingly took the lead as soon as Dan waved. Rocky followed when Fay arrived safely at the bottom, then it was my turn, once Rocky had made it down.

The surrounding snow gums had in some nearby places been uprooted from the ground by either a rockslide or a massive avalanche of snow. After tethering our horses, Jimmie led us through this tangle to a relatively open space. 'He be in there,' Jimmie said confidently, pointing to an accumulation of logs.

'I must go first,' Dan said, stepping forward. 'After all, I do formally represent the law, and it's my responsibility to identify this scoundrel.

'Once I've ascertained it's Bamford, I'll wave, and you can all present your yourselves if you wish.'

Barely a minute lapsed before Dan emerged from that jumble of logs and signalled.

As Rocky, Fay, Jimmie and I filed past Dan, he said. 'He's in there all right. If you've got a handkerchief, use it, he stinks to high heaven. And I think he's blind and he's definitely lost all his teeth ... not a pretty sight.'

Dan wasn't joking, the refuge Bamford had chosen was putrid, yet the more shocking presence was Bamford, just a human shell, almost a cadaver and clearly close to death.

'If you can hear me Bamford, just nod your head,' Rocky said, his voiced raised enough to override Bamford's mumbling and snivelling. Bamford nodded, albeit without much enthusiasm.

'It's me, Rocky. You remember me, don't you?'

Bamford flinched, blinked furiously then fully opened his opaque, sightless eyes. I think we all heard him say, something like, 'Thank God, I'm saved. Please, mate, yah gotta get me out of here ... away from those black devils who haunt me bloody day and night.'

'Bamford, I never was, and never will be your mate.' Rocky responded calmy, but loud enough for all to hear.

'And I have no intention of saving your grubby arse, not even after you confess to Jim Barclay's murder. You see, Bamford, nobody murders my friends and can expect to get away with it. Before these witnesses, you no-good piece of shit, tell me why you murdered Jim!'

'Promised me a fifty-fifty deal, on the sale of all the cattle we duffed and managed on his station. But 'e reneged ... and that bastard dog of his bit me. Now, yah gotta get me outa 'ere ... please ... please Rocky; before I die.'

'Never! You shot my friend in the back, Bamford. And that's enough of your snivelling. I hope your mother once loved you, because no one else on this earth ever has.'

There was a click as Rocky cocked his handgun.

Bang!

We watched in shock, I suppose, as Bamford twitched once as he slumped to the ground leaving a mess of hair, bone, brains and blood sliding down the log which only seconds before had been his backrest.

'That's the same murdering bastard who had wanted to kill you not that long ago Leon,' Rocky said as smoke rose from the barrel of his six-shooter. 'And what's even more despicable, he was partly responsible for Adam's unnecessary death.'

Bamford had been in a bad way physically—and mentally it must be said. Nevertheless, we were all now party to murder. I felt no grief, other than for Rocky.

'C'mon, it's time to get out of here,' Dan ordered. 'But first, help me drag some of these logs over his body. Not *ever* a word to anyone about this ... and you have my word that my report will not include what just transpired. Understood!?

'Hopefully, he'll remain a missing person.'

* * *

Unfortunately, Dan's parting words were not meant to be.

A few months later, while on patrol searching the high plains country for miscreants, three policemen came upon a booted foot poking from beneath a random stack of logs. The body was taken to Dargo, about eighty miles from where it was found, and later, buried in the cemetery there.

A postmortem revealed a bullet lodged in the skull of one, Mr John Bamford.

During the inquest which followed, a verdict of murder by person or persons unknown was handed down.

31

We returned to our campsite near Grant. The campfire was soon crackling enthusiastically, our horses were given a quick brushing and set loose to browse with our two pack horses. Tea was prepared and as soon as Jimmie and Dan had each downed two mugs of very sweetened brew, they set off to meet with the local indigenous mob.

The news when they returned about three hours later was not good.

'That Mickey fella, he not be seen by my mob for last two weeks,' Jimmie explained. 'But, three fellas who come this way, up from Sale with sheep for selling to butcher here, reckon they saw him at the pub in Dargo.'

'And later see him getting on a coach, leaving town, Dan added. 'Pissed as a parrot and next stop at Bairnsdale.'

'Bugger!' Fay swore. 'That means he could be going either east, west or south, or leaving by ship to God only knows where.'

I expected Rocky to show some anger that the trail to Mickey had gone cold, but there was none, but rather, a thoughtful frown creased his forehead.

'Then that smart arse butcher here might know a thing or two,'

Fay suggested cheekily. 'Didn't you tell me, darling, that Bamford and Mickey left Grant in quite a hurry, and, without paying for an order of beef they sort of demanded?'

'Yep. That's right,' I said, while nodding. 'That serves him right I reckon. He's not the most pleasant chap.'

'Then our first order of the day,' Rocky chimed in, 'will be to pay a visit to that butcher; real early like.'

* * *

THE FOLLOWING MORNING: that unique time of the false dawn.

Jimmie had kicked our campfire back into life, providing sufficient light to get the billies boiling and to organise a light breakfast. It was also bloody cold, and none of us were overly keen to leave the warmth of our fire; but duty called.

In quick order we hauled on our wool lined jackets, saddled our horses then hobbled the pack horses.

Riding into town was pleasant enough; day breaking, the muted sounds of humanity commencing its daily routine, the smell of smoke and the occasional dog or two barking in protest at not having been fed.

Arriving at the butcher shop, our luck was in. The butcher was in attendance, and we could see him through the shop's front window lighting one of his lanterns.

We all dismounted, tethered our horses then briskly followed Rocky into the shop, disregarding that the front door was closed.

'Hey! Yah's can't just barge in like that! Can't yah see I'm not open for business? Go on! Allus yah, piss off.'

'And top of the morning to you too, sir,' I smiled and replied cheekily.

'You'll no doubt remember me, but I do apologise; I can't recall your name.'

'Yeah, I remember, but I'll tell you again, I aint letting no Abo's inta me shop.'

Taking advantage that the butcher was at the far end of the shop,

I quickly leant over the counter, and as luck would have it, soon found and removed the shot gun I knew resided there. 'So you say, sir, but that's against the law and as you can see, one of these gentlemen represents that law.'

Waving the shotgun around, I added, 'You can have this back when we leave, but in the meantime, we'd just like to have a friendly chat. So, I'd suggest you relax and cooperate ... and answer our questions, truthfully like. OK?'

'For starters,' said Rocky, 'I understand you know John Bamford and that bloke, Mickey. We know Bamford's whereabouts, and that Mickey has left Grant. We just want you to tell us Mickey's whereabouts.'

'But before you answer, sir,' I interrupted, 'we also understand they both left Grant owing you a considerable amount of money.'

'So, to make our time here as brief as possible,' Dan added, 'exactly how much was involved in their fraud?'

'I have a record in me logbook; I'll get it.'

'Excellent idea,' Dan replied. 'But I'll come with you while you do so.'

The butcher lobbed his notebook onto the counter.

Fay swooped to pick it up, and no more than thirty seconds passed before she announced, 'Thirty-seven quid and twenty shillings. Not an amount to be sneezed at. Is this the unpaid amount you claim?'

'Yes, it is,' our friendly butcher replied.

In a heartbeat, Rocky threw forty quid onto the counter. 'You get to keep that if you answer our questions.

'Right, let's get started.'

'Look, I really don't have much to say,' the butcher replied, 'other than that I've heard a few rumours. It's been bandied about a bit that Mickey was headed for a place called, Dorrigo. I've no idea where that is though; somewhere in New South Wales, I think.'

'If you're bullshitting us, you can expect another visit by us,' Dan said calmly, 'and it'll be jailtime for you I can assure you. Got any names regarding active bushrangers?'

Our butcher friend just shrugged his shoulders and said. 'Nah, just rumours. Nail one or two and you'll get all the answers you want. But, right now, you'll be wasting your time.'

'How's business, sir,' I asked cautiously, wanting to change the subject slightly.

'Bad, there's no cattle left here, and none scheduled to come this way in the foreseeable future. And you can forget any idea of buying lamb or pork, the prices are too high.

'And it's all your fault! Nobody's yet replaced those two to continue the trade, like.'

'You mean *illegal trade*, I'm sure,' Rocky reminded our friend. 'And the risk of obtaining fresh meat legally up here is not worth it; right?'

'Yeah, that, and the gold's starting to run out, which means the "insolvents track" back to city life is becoming a bushranger's gold mine.'

'Thank you for that information, sir, and do you know what?' Dan asked. 'I think I believe you, so I'll discuss this with my senior when I return to Wangaratta.'

'I don't give a bugger what you think and do, sonny boy. I'm getting out of this dump very shortly. Maybe I'll find my way to Dorrigo and catch up with Mickey. Perhaps he can find a job for me. Ha, ha, bloody ha.'

'I'd stay away from Dorrigo if I were you,' Rocky replied, there being no mistaking his threat. 'OK. Take your money, and here's yah shotgun. Keep yah nose clean, and if I hear you're operating anywhere, illegal like, yah won't get a good word from any of us to help save yah neck.'

'And if we ever have to meet again, whatever your name is,' Fay suddenly interjected, unable to hide her disgust of this bloke, 'please tub up, or at least have a swim beforehand ... and show some decency; at least button up your trouser fly.'

'Oh, young lady, that's very observant of you I must say. There's a decent one down there all right, but fear not, a dead bird never falls from the nest.'

Fay's prude-like attitude suddenly gave way to raucous laughter, leaving me just a tad embarrassed, until Rocky and Dan joined the levity. Which goes to show, even dodgy operators and criminals can possess a sense of humour.

* * *

We all dutifully returned safely and unscathed to our respective homes.

Discouragingly, we had to wait another eighteen months before receiving confirmation that Mickey was in fact living in the vicinity of Dorrigo, practising the only art he was any good at: cattle duffing.

32

Eighteen months flew by, though not without incident.

The saddest issue which presented itself was the chronic painful condition of Rocky's ageing legs and his lower back, both of which worsened rapidly not long after our return from Grant. He confided in me that he had visited a doctor in Wangaratta seeking any kind of pain relief—which he received—but also received "an unwelcome doctor's opinion" ... that he had also recently experienced a mild stroke. That advice included advising Rocky that he had to slow down, which did not sit well with him; in fact, he was thoroughly pissed off.

Yet, with typical stoicism, Rocky accepted his situation, seldom complaining, and on a few occasions accepted my arm to help him navigate the stairs to and from the front veranda.

At the end of a day's hard work, Fay and I nevertheless got many opportunities to sit with Rocky (usually after dinner, in the evening when the flies had retired and before the mosquitos launched their unwelcome attacks) and discuss our achievements. He never failed to compliment us and had a way of suggesting how to conserve our energy by sharing tasks, evade snakes and avoid being stung by the dreaded "jack jumper" bull ants ... without ever big noting himself.

His stories fascinated us, revealing a side to his nature at which he had only hinted at previously: of the time when he first arrived in Australia, and growing up in northeast Victoria.

Those stories revealed a man possessed of low tolerance of other men who deliberately either disadvantaged or tried to stand over, or bully less fortunate others.

'More than once, I intervened to warn blokes to back off from antagonising hard-working farmers,' Rocky said in a matter-of-fact manner, 'You know, like when a poor bugger farmer was struggling a bit and overdue in repaying a small debt.

'Or, when defusing a dispute over selling unbranded cattle which had wandered from one property to another. I've done that exact same thing over many years, with nothing more than a handshake between long-established high-country graziers. No fuss, and all remain good friends, except of course Jim Barclay, who was murdered by that bastard Bamford.

'If any of my unbranded cattle were to wander onto any of the leaseholds adjacent to mine, they would be sold on my behalf to save me the time, effort and trouble of separately finding, removing and branding those cattle. I'd receive cash money for that stock, plus paperwork to prove the auction sale prices. With Adam's help, we faithfully reciprocated that agreement with our neighbours and things evened-out over time.

'Regardless, back in those days, occasionally some smart arsed new bloke would turn up wanting to buck the system and reckoned they had a right to square the head count ledger at any time, with force, if need be.

'So, when a quiet chat over a cuppa failed to reach agreement, unresolved problems were solved using me fists. I was useful in that art, and several blokes regretted taking me on. I'd then send 'em packing, with a final warning, reminding 'em, 'that I never start fights; I just finish 'em'.

Mind you, now studying Rocky's old, but still well-muscled frame and bulk, it was easy to imagine his youthful, formidable stature, and that that alone should have warned his adversaries to reconsider their objections to the prevailing high country stock recognition and ownership agreement.

Whether working or living with Rocky, or when in the company of neighbours, or shop owners in Wangaratta, he was always respectful and generously helped struggling farmers and their families, with an eye to reducing local crime ... despite being engaged in questionable cattle dealings of his own.

* * *

Never at the exclusion of Rocky, most of those warm summer evenings on the front veranda also provided opportunities for Fay and me to yarn with my stepparents, Elspeth and Max.

With a lingering sadness, their son, Bertie, seemed determined to remain private and distant. Regardless, Elspeth and Max maintained that the best thing in their lives was moving to Australia, and how proud they were of me and Fay ... which in turn gave me the opportunity to express my appreciation for their unfaltering care and interest in my maturity.

Mind you, they never missed an opportunity to either hint at or express their only regret; that Fay and I were then childless.

* * *

Not all those family gatherings were idle chatter. Max, but more so, Elspeth, loved playing cards, and we all knew we were in for a bit of fun and a lot of laughs whenever Elspeth arrived carrying her box of playing cards.

Both were very good players, whereas Fay and I were "easy beats".

It must have been frustrating for Elspeth because she had met her match in Rocky, who somehow repeatedly either trumped her, or drew incredible winning hands in poker.

During a tea break, Max good naturedly challenged Rocky. 'I

know you wouldn't cheat, so you must nevertheless have an incredibly lucky streak going on. Do yah reckon it'll ever run out?'

'Only when I fall off the perch,' Rocky replied cheekily. 'It's more to do with studying your opponent's little habits and a lifetime spent getting to know what to expect from the fall of the cards.

'That's how I got to own this property and this homestead. There was nothing dodgy about how I won a tight card game. Plus, there were several witnesses. And there's no rules or law about *not* studying your opponent beforehand. That gentleman had a well-known, overblown ego, and was three parts pissed. He didn't really have a chance of beating me, his decisions were pitiful, and ultimately, extremely embarrassing for him.

'I've never seen or heard of him since the day he handed over the property papers and the house door keys.

'So, remember this piece of advice my dear friends; never drink alcohol before going to the races ... or before playing cards for money.'

* * *

IT WAS during those evening gatherings which included Elspeth and Max that Rocky reminisced how Adam came into his life, how their unique business operations had developed so covertly, how they explored the high country together and how it came to be that Rocky treated Adam as his own son.

That was no doubt a fulfilling time, but there was yet another reality governing Adam's way through life, and beyond, for he was revered by his local mob ... for reasons that will probably forever remain a secret.

* * *

ONE PARTICULARLY BALMY EVENING, well after the moon had set, Fay stood, yawned and then said, 'thanks Mum and Dad, I've had such a lovely evening, but I've got to get some sleep.'

I too stood, stretched, stifled my own yawn and said casually. 'Well, my darling girl, are you going to tell them, or will I?'

'Oh yes, I almost forgot,' Fay faked surprise with equal planned casualness. 'It so happens I'm pregnant.'

33

Inspired by the imminent arrival of our first child, and parenthood, my feelings for Fay took on an additional but different fascination, and a powerful need to be her provider and protector.

Many times, I glanced at her, never tiring of the introspective pleasure I received because she was so beguilingly beautiful: glances, never staring, because I didn't want her to think I was making fun of her increasingly rotund condition.

Consistently however, she would catch me out and return the most wonderful, contented smile; a playful blend of "caught yah", and "aren't we just so damn smart"!

The choice of a name for our child was easy. We agreed immediately, if a boy then it would be Adam. But, if a girl, Charlotte, that being Elspeth's middle name.

* * *

Life continued serenely.

When conditions permitted, we regularly opted to sleep outside in our sleeping bags. To slowly come awake to a cool, misty morning free of the torment of flies and mosquitoes, plus an enchanting cacophony of bird calls welcoming the new day and the occasional call of nearby cattle, made me realise how much I loved where we lived.

'Leon my darling, it really is the most beautiful time of day,' Fay would typically say in a low, husky voice, usually surprising me that she had wakened before me.

Regardless, my first reply was always, 'are you OK?'

'If I'm not, it's your fault you know that don't you?'

* * *

Despite Fay's condition she worked hard, side-by-side with me during most mornings, helping to repair and replace fencing, and install new, properly hinged iron gates. However, come midday, she would retreat to the shade of the house and sleep until well into the afternoon.

Early one evening, not long after I'd arrived back at the house, Rocky arrived driving his favourite, two-seater buggy.

'Good God you two, don't you ever stop working?'

'Only if one of us gets bitten by a nest of jack jumpers,' Fay replied mischievously. 'So, how do we honour this visitation, kind sir?'

'By listening carefully to what I've got to say,' Rocky said rather sharply, 'but not until we have a cuppa and some of that barley sugar which Elspeth denies me. I know you're hiding some!'

As Rocky prepared to step from the buggy, I grabbed the horse's reins and loosely tied them to a nearby sapling. 'Hold yah flow Rocky,' I called quickly, 'let me give you a hand; can't have yah goin' arse overhead.'

Barely had Rocky negotiated the front steps did he plant himself into one of our old wicker chairs, when Fay arrived with his request. She filled his favourite mug with steaming hot tea, then offered him a plate of freshly baked fruitcake and several chunks of barley sugar.

'Thanks Fay, you're one in a million,' Rocky said, genuinely impressed with her thoughtfulness, but quickly corrected himself. 'Actually, you're one and a half in a million, eh.'

'Flattery will get you everything, mate,' I interrupted, 'so what is it that's got you so excited?

'Thought you'd never ask,' Rocky replied after blowing a long breath over the surface of his cuppa.

'I've got a couple of things I need to tell you; to get them off me chest, like.

'The first is a personal matter; my decision while I've still got all me marbles. As you no doubt know, it was my intention to leave this property to Adam. He was keen to legally improve our herd, amongst many other things, but that was snatched from him by that lousy bastard who needlessly killed him.

'However, if you are happy to do me a great honour, would you both, instead, accept my inheritance? You're more than capable of carrying on what's needed to be done around here,' said Rocky in his matter-of-fact manner, pausing as he rummaged for something inside his over-jacket.

Somewhat theatrically, and smiling conspiratorially, he suddenly produced a bundle of papers from his jacket. 'Here, you'll need these,' he said as he thrust the papers into my hand.

'We'll need to visit my solicitor, in Wang, to legally transfer ownership, now, rather than after I've stepped off me perch. I really want to spend some time with my grandkids; you know, like teachin 'em how to fish and to ride of course.

'So, by the dumbfounded looks on your faces, that'll be a *yes* then?'

Fay was on her feet in a flash, both hands in fists upon her chest, her mouth wide open. 'But, but ... oh dear God, Rocky you darling sneaky old bugger, of course that's a yes,' she said, tears already miraculously rolling down her cheeks. In just two steps she had Rocky in her arms, and would you believe it, our tough, kind mentor was similarly afflicted.

I too was shocked and overjoyed, but all I did was walk up behind

Rocky and put him in a headlock. 'Thanks heaps, Rocky,' I whispered in his ear, 'we'll do you proud, you'll see.'

Had you been a fly on the wall, I suppose seeing three crying, hugging adults would have been a bit strange.

But that mood was soon about to change.

'You're always full of surprises Rocky,' I acknowledged, while drying my eyes on my shirtsleeves, 'but you said there were two bits of news. Surely there's nothing that'll top what you've just done for us?'

'Well, that depends upon how you look at things, Leon. I've just received information about Mickey's precise whereabouts. I *will* get him—eventually—and he *will* pay the price.'

34

___

Oh yes, Rocky had a plan or two in mind alright.

However, by necessity, a few months lapsed before they could be implemented. Foremost, were considerations around Fay's health over the next two months, and obviously immediately those following the scheduled arrival of our first child.

Elspeth and Max were a step ahead of everyone, for they had already transformed an unused homestead bedroom into a nursery. And, upon their insistence, Fay and I were to move back to the homestead, *just in case.*

More judicious tasks followed. First, Rocky wanted a private chat with his understanding and loyal friend, Senior Constable Don Carmichael, in Wangaratta. He felt compelled, for all concerned, to explain his intentions to locate and arrest Mickey, and escort him back to Wang to answer some serious charges ranging from numerous acts of cattle duffing, monetary theft, planning to commit fraud, aiding and abetting murder, and of course, Adam's death.

I accompanied Rocky on that visit and after a few brief words of mutual endearment, and handshakes all around, we got straight to the point.

'Once again, Rocky, my dear friend,' Don said after contemplating what he'd just heard. 'I sympathise with your worthy objectives. However, if you undertake to bring Mickey back here, unharmed, then you have my blessings and support.

'I'll provide you with a letter authorising you to call upon the help of the New South Wales boys in blue to render whatever assistance you might need. So, from today until you finish this job, you will both be empowered to make arrests as you see fit.

'And to cover both our arses, I'll also write to the Victorian Police Commissioner explaining my decision to take advantage of the opportunity you have afforded me. I'll also be using that opportunity to underscore my plea for more trained officers for our region.

'So, will it be just you and Leon on this deployment?'

'Actually, no. I was hoping you could talk again to your counterpart in Warrnambool to release officer Dan Cameron to give us a hand; he's a damn good man to have around.'

'Understood. I'll move on that immediately, but I can't guarantee anything. Mind you, I've ear marked him as my replacement, so I'll welcome having him around here again for a while.

'So then Rocky, how do you propose to get to Dorrigo, and to move about once you get there? You're too bloody old to be doing this; I told you that last time we met.'

'We've got that sorted. I *can* still ride,' Rocky replied just a bit indignant like.

'The three of us will make our way north and catch the train to Sydney and then transfer to another train that'll take us onto Newcastle. Our horses will be with us on both trains ... and then we ride to Dorrigo. As soon as we arrive, I'll buy or rent a buggy, something common place that won't attract attention and then rent a house away from the main street.

'We'll avoid being seen together as much as possible. I'll mostly stay in the house while Leon and Dan move around the town making enquiries which might lead us to Mickey.'

'Well, go on Leon, tell Don what else you've thought about.'

'Mickey would probably recognise Rocky and me, so, starting

from today, we've agreed to disguise ourselves in the hope that we can find Mickey before he lays eyes on one of us and clears out.

'We'll not be shaving between now and when we nail Mickey, and, before we return to Rocky's farm today, we're going to buy very different clothing and boots than that which we usually wear. By the time we arrive in Dorrigo, those items will appear well broken in, and not attract any attention, even if we were to walk straight past Mickey.'

'Yeah, right; not bad thinking Leon, I'm impressed,' Don replied, but quickly added, 'I don't suppose you'd consider a career as a copper one day?'

'Who knows, Don, maybe if Dan takes up your offer first,' I recall replying.

'I'll remember that Leon,' Don replied, smiling to himself as if he had just caught a two-pound rainbow trout. 'Here, you'll need these, and don't, for God's sake lose this key.'

That meeting over, Rocky and I went shopping, both of us for new clothes and boots, and I for some flowers for Fay.

Our return trip was companionable, occasionally interrupted by the jangle of the handcuffs now suspended from my trousers belt.

* * *

As if the care and attention that Fay and the baby would receive from Elspeth and Max wouldn't be adequate, Max put the word around with our neighbours that he and Elspeth wanted to hire "a live-in housekeeper with a range of domestic skills and baby-sitting experience".

Not only did the very first applicant succeed, but a "special condition" accompanied that woman's employment; that her husband might from time-to-time need to chip in and help with any heavy work!

These folk, Anna and Fred Portesi, were in fact our second closest neighbours. Both struggled with English, just as we tried to grasp Italian, and on several occasions, we had to stop what we were doing and have a cuppa before having another go at understanding each other. Great laughter and exaggerated over usage of strange words or phrases would follow, but with patience, we eventually began to learn a lot about each other. Not surprisingly, our families became lifelong friends, and my word, were they good workers.

Regardless, Max had chosen well. Anna turned out to be a great cook and had every right to be proud of her many beautiful pasta dishes with which she plied us, usually for Sunday lunch.

She had reared five children of her own. Fay not only adored her but spent hours swapping stories about Italy, and Australia and it wasn't long before Fay knew the names of all her children, and close family members she'd left behind in northern Italy.

Anna even drew Elspeth out of her comfort zone, by teaching her how to sing a few festive Italian songs. On more than one occasion, Rocky, Fred and I, accompanied by a bottle or two of wine, would join in. Fred, I have to say, had the most fantastic voice, and it took little encouragement to get him singing solo renditions of his many lost lovers.

Fred, only half the size of Anna, loved being outdoors and knew his way around cattle which was exactly what was needed while Rocky and I attempted to bring Mickey to justice.

And, by the way, Fred grew grapes on his property, 'alla whicha made da besta vino; no grappa, you unnerstan?' Over time, the old bugger turned me into a lover of his fantastic home-made organic Durif wine.

* * *

LATE ONE AFTERNOON as I was returning to the homestead after a successful session of trout fishing, when Jimmie, my local aboriginal "brother", casually stepped in front of me, frightening the hell out of me because, honest to God, I had not seen him standing stationary next to the track I was walking on.

'Bloody hell, Jimmie, it's good to see you, but where'd you come from!?' I said shakily, trying to shrug off the shock I'd just experienced.

'I teach you how, one day, eh? I just passin' coz I see you an' Rocky goin' after that Mickey bloke.'

'Well, yes, we are, but how do you know that? I've not told anybody away from this place, other than the copper in Wang, and he wants it kept secret as much as Rocky and I do.

'That be somethin' else I maybe teach you later.

'When you three be leavin' Leon?'

'As soon as Fay has our baby; she's due in about two months' time.'

'Yes, that be good news about child for you Leon an' Fay. All my mob happy.'

'Thanks Jimmie, but hang on, how do you know there'll be three of us going after Mickey?'

'That easy nuff. Dan! He send me message short time ago saying he returning to Wang soon, to help you and Rocky.

'When you leave, I'll see that nothing happens Fay or child. I go now; good seeing you again Leon.'

'Thanks Jimmie, you're a good brother. Here, take these fish, I caught them only an hour ago.'

'Don't mind if I do, but you shoulda landed thata big brown trout, they best eating. Sometimes you slow learner Leon.'

EVERYTHING WE'D PLANNED, to date, was falling easily into place ... except that Fay had the strangest notion she and our child were not going to be left out of our pursuit of that mad bastard, Mickey.

Thank God for Anna, for she recalled a few delusional episodes during a couple of her own pre and post deliveries and set about counselling Fay which included making her realise that her job was to focus upon nurturing our child, not putting it at risk.

The extent to which Anna succeeded became evident after we returned from our upcoming deployment.

35

Charlotte's arrival was an amazing event. I felt the pain and anxiety which Fay endured to start our family. I also felt a most unexpected surge of relief, pride and excitement when Fay handed our daughter to me.

That tiny, pinkish purple bundle never screamed, or squirmed, or peed all over me as some suggested would happen. And to this day I not only remember the way she looked at me with her deep dark eyes and smiled at me as if we'd known each other for ages ... but who then reached out a chubby little hand and latched onto my thumb.

Did I imagine a calm faint voice that said, 'all will be great dad, just wait and see.' Yeah, I guess I did imagine it, but I did feel something when she contentedly closed her eyes to sleep: it was Fay's hand resting lightly on my arm.

I was suddenly rendered breathless, but Fred Portesi placed one of his arms around my shoulders and said quietly, 'Your life witha Fay, it really only starts anow Leon. Embraysa thisa moment because God has just handed you lovely people hisa greatest gift ... a gift more important thana your owna lives.'

* * *

Rocky too was so proud, and between jobs made any excuse to seek out Charlotte and either cuddle her, bounce her on his knees or, despite Fay's initial protestations, carefully place her on the back of his favourite waler, or take her for a short ride in his buggy.

Many years later I quizzed Charlotte if she remembered who it was that did all those things with her. Without hesitation she answered, 'of course Dad, that was grandpa Rocky. And I bet what you and Mum don't know, is that Rocky always saved some of his barley sugar just for me.'

* * *

As planned, about a month after Charlotte's birth, all was in readiness for our quest to locate and arrest Mickey.

Officer Dan Cameron, our police escort and close aboriginal friend had arrived with a fully kitted out packhorse and was breaking his neck to meet our daughter.

'Bloody hell Leon, she's beautiful mate. Just as well Fay has some good looks. I'll bet Charlotte will fit in nicely with my two upstarts; mind you, they're not bad kids really.'

'It's great to see you too Dan, but just one question. How did you know about Charlotte?'

'Too easy my friend, I regularly keep in touch with Jimmie. I thought you knew that. And didn't Jimmie recently promise you he was going to teach you our little trick?'

* * *

It took another two days to assemble everything we'd need for our expedition: our best walers (all having been re-shod a fortnight previously), saddles and bridles, sleeping bags, wide brimmed hats, clothing, both new and old, handguns and ammunition, money and food etc, spare boots, a variety of six bottles of Fred's excellent wines, towels and a few basic toiletries ... but deliberately, *no* shaving gear.

Rocky, though restricted by his chronic back and leg pain, nevertheless did what he could to assist without getting in the way. He had little to say during this time, it being clear to me he had something weighing heavily upon his thoughts.

It wasn't that he'd misplaced Senior Don Carmichael's letter, perhaps it was that he had forgotten to organise tickets for our train journey. No, it wasn't that either, and, I had no intention of pressing him to come clean; I'd find out in due course what was plaguing him.

Fay, though caught up in our excitement somewhat, was still a bit grumpy as we finally departed Rocky's property. The early morning air was cool, and little was talked about which had not been discussed multiple times previously. Lack of determination to succeed with our plans was never in question.

When I turned in my saddle to blow a kiss to Fay, and give my parting farewell wave to Max, Elspeth and Anna, there was Charlotte, rugged up to the nines in Fay's arms, her little arms flapping about (with Fay's assistance) waving to me and giving me the best of her toothless smiles. Fay too, was now smiling perplexingly, once again leaving me breathless when she suddenly poked her tongue out at me.

36

Having travelled only a few miles, Rocky suggested an immediate change to our plans. 'It'll now be too damn risky to use any of the high-country tracks that would take us northward. As yah can see, unfortunately it looks like we're in for a decent rainstorm; and this little event could last for days.'

He wasn't joking, the weather was about to suddenly and unexpectedly turn, a characteristic well known to occur in Victoria's northeast. Not only had the clouds quickly changed from a whiteish grey, to almost black, but a sporadic wind sprang up, unnerving our horses somewhat as each new gust hit us, each stronger and colder than its predecessor.

'C'mon lads,' Rocky shouted as he kicked his mount into a rolling canter with which his packhorse could keep pace. 'Hang onto your hats and let's get moving. We're going to need shelter, and soon like.'

'Hey, Rocky,' I shouted, just as the first flicker of lightning ran to earth, followed by a distant rumble of thunder. 'We'll probably get saturated whatever we do, but that bridge which crosses the Buckland River isn't more than half a mile from here. We should all be able to shelter beneath it I reckon.

'OK Leon, you lead,' Rocky shouted and gestured impatiently, 'and let's hope there's no hailstones before we get there.'

The ever-pragmatic constable Cameron added, 'and let's hope we can get out from under the bridge before the bloody river rises too much.'

Yes, we all got saturated, and there was ample space beneath the bridge. Regardless, the river water was already becoming turbid and rising, albeit slowly at that stage.

We could hear the storm approaching, and intensifying, at least ten minutes before it arrived and threw its full force upon our position.

Moderate rain, then small hail and then huge hailstones made it impossible to hear what anyone was saying as they clattered on top of the bridge, and noisily stripped leaves and small branches from the surrounding foliage.

Shortly after, the wind, which had been at worst, annoying, suddenly became ferocious, even lifting some of the thick planks which formed the bridge's surface.

It seemed, as if not to be outdone, that the arrival of persistent flashes of forked lightning and horrendously loud claps of thunder had conspired to frighten the bejesus out of us: which on occasions it certainly did.

Of course, this savage onset of nature's forces tested the equanimity of our walers, but incredibly, none panicked and responded amazingly well to our constant efforts to keep them calm. (Just another example of the mazing temperament of Rocky's walers.)

Typical of such weather events, the storm stopped as quickly as it had started, leaving a remarkable silence only interrupted by raindrops striking the ground after being shed from the surrounding trees.

'I suggest we leave here, like right now,' Dan said loudly as he exaggeratedly pointed to the river.

Focussing upon the river, I involuntarily gasped in shock. Before us, the Buckland River was now visibly rising and a dark brown, frightening torrent of water, tree roots, tea-tree scrub, fence posts and fencing wire, and two calves which had not long ago drowned.

Rocky hadn't wasted any time or needed any advice; he was already mounted and urging his horses up onto the road leading onto the bridge. Dan and I rapidly followed.

'I've never in my life copped anything quite like that,' Rocky reminisced, 'but we must keep moving while this break permits. 'Shelter's still our priority so I suggest we try and make it into Wang before nightfall.'

Though that inclement weather layover under the bridge was a little scary, it also had elements of embarrassment and frustration. We should have responded more quickly because it was obvious the weather was about to change for the worst; the result being that we got saturated. And, that it started to bucket down when we were only three or four miles from Wang resulted a second and more uncomfortable drenching.

Rocky saved the day, calling on a friend, Alan Watts, who owed him a favour or two. With all four of us working frantically in the rain, we soon had our swags and saddle bags heaped on the floor of an old, but tidy barn. Fortuitously, the long drop toilet was close by.

While the barn kept the freezing cold wind at bay, alas, the roof was not without a few annoyingly positioned leaks.

Alan plied us with mugs of hot black tea, several blankets, old pillows and then filled the four pressure lanterns which were strategically placed on each wall. 'Give me yah wettest clothes, and yah boots,' he volunteered. 'I've got a fire going inside and I'll do me best to dry 'em out for yah by morning.

'Sorry about there being no beds, but you can pull apart as many of those hay bales as you like; that might make things a bit more comfortable. And, oh yes, there's five good buckets in here somewhere. Use 'em to catch the worst of the leaks.'

'Thanks Alan, we'll make do,' replied Rocky, 'but have you got somewhere we can put our horses out of the wind and rain, like?'

'Yep, there's a three-sided lean-to attached to the back, and in fact, its roof is in better condition than this 'ere barn.'

Dan and I dashed outside during a brief let up in the rain and led our six horses into their shelter for the night. Inside were ten large stalls, the floors of which had recently been covered generously with reasonably fresh straw.

We moved quickly relieving each horse of its saddle, bridle or halter, then led them each into their own stall.

'By the way lads,' 'said Alan, 'there's oats and chaff in those bags up against the back wall and you'll find a scoop in each bag. I've found that one scoop of oats tah two of chaff is about right. Perhaps a bit more if that doesn't fill their feed boxes; that's them hanging on the right-hand side wall of each stall.'

'Did you hear that my boys? You're having oats and chaff for dinner; not bad, thanks to Alan,' I rattled on, unnecessarily adding, 'it's going to be bloody cold overnight, you lot,' so, be patient and eat up while I go get your coats.'

* * *

THE LEAK CATCHING BUCKETS, though provided with honest good intent by Alan, were a disaster. It wasn't because they didn't do their job, they did. But when one is on the abyss of deep sleep, there can be nothing more aggravating than trying not to become victim to the Chinese Torture of dripping water striking the surface of a part full bucket, let alone five of them.

But perhaps that torture *was* trumped that night: being dry, comfortable, finally warm, and about to drop into that beckoning sleep abyss, to realise that soon, yet again, it was your turn to empty those goddam buckets before they overflowed.

Dan and I had agreed Rocky would be exempted from that task, and to justify that decision, in the morning we both had to not only help extract him from his swag but pull up his trousers and boots.

'Thanks lads, I have to admit simple things like that are getting more difficult by the day,' he said, I suspect a little embarrassed; but he still had the cheek to mischievously add, 'mind you, I slept rather well, how about you two?'

37

———————

Two days later the rain and wind finally eased and then abated. We were bored, but that was ample time for our clothes and gear to dry out.

Our luck turned.

We were soon able to exercise our horses, and then left them to feed on lush grass in the paddock adjacent to Alan's homestead.

When Rocky was coping better with the pain in his lower back, we ventured into the Wangaratta railway station to formalise arrangements to transport our horses to Sydney and beyond, not suspecting what eventuated.

'You blokes are in luck, that's for sure,' the Station Master assured us. 'The Ovens River has flooded for miles around, but the rail line hasn't been impacted, not yet anyway.

'Not just that, but there's been cancellations. If you can get your horses here by not later than half past four this arvo, then your nags can have an entire carriage to themselves, though I can't guarantee that beyond Albury. That change of trains is necessary because the New South Wales rail gauge differs from ours. My guess is that that will take about half an hour.

'I've also checked the North bound Timetable from Sydney to

Newcastle. It's reasonably reliable, but you won't have to change trains again. However, there'll be a stop-over for about an hour in Sydney, to load other northbound folk. That's usually enough time to get a good meal at the Sydney station, and for you to freshen yourselves up a bit.'

'So, what's the damage mate?' Rocky politely asked.

'From Wang to Albury, the best I can do is five quid per horse, including water and feed; plus, two quid each for you blokes, which includes storing your gear and saddles, and so on.

'You can sit wherever you like in one of the paying customer carriages. Mind you though, I'd suggest you bring along a blanket or two and a pillow. It gets a bit drafty in there as you'll soon discover.'

'It's a deal. Here's forty quid; and thanks for your assistance,' said Rocky as he shook hands with the Station Master. 'I trust you'll not skip the country before we return.' We all chuckled in good humour as we retreated from the station.

However, all mirth quickly evaporated when the Station Master sheepishly called out to us. 'There's a bit of not so good news boys. My counterpart in Albury will probably relieve you of at least triple that.'

* * *

CONTENT AND SOMEWHAT EXCITED, we were soon back at Alan's homestead. We felt no obligation or resentment towards Rocky for sitting down while Dan and I rounded up our horses, brushed them off, curry combed their backs and legs, and then started packing our belongings.

It was during this time that Dan found three small, brown paper wrapped parcels. 'Hey, have a look at this; a surprise, one each, I guess. And Alan's left a note; here's what he says.'

Thanks for calling by. Nice meeting you Leon, and Dan. Good luck with whatever you're up to, but take care. The soap I make myself. See if you can pick what it smells like. No clues. See over.

"Redgum after rain"

Indeed, a thoughtful bloke that, and he had certainty nailed the soap's fragrance.

* * *

AFTER A SHORT TEA BREAK, we fitted saddles, bridle's, halters and swags to our horses and tidied up the barn and the lean-to.

Having helped Rocky into his saddle, he handed me three, ten-pound notes. 'Be a good lad Leon,' he said. 'Whack a nail through these and leave 'em hangin' where Alan will find 'em.'

* * *

THE EVENTS of the past few days were blessings in disguise. Had we attempted to cross the mountains to save time, we'd probably have had to turn back, and for absolute certain, we'd not be feeling as relaxed and rested as we, and no doubt our horses were, right then.

What's more, given our unexpected good luck in catching a train so easily, we were now days ahead of our original, over-optimistic plans.

After a small amount of shunting to minimise the effort to load our horses, a whistle shrieked and after a jolt as the carriage linkages took up any slack between them ... we were underway, and on-time as dictated by the Victorian Railways Timetable.

We were the only passengers in our chosen carriage, but it wasn't long before we realised the seating arrangements left a lot to be desired ... next to no seat padding and it was drafty and becoming bloody cold. Rocky, though not outwardly appearing to be a bit under the weather, made no protest when Dan and I both volunteered one of our blankets for him.

Regardless, it concerned me his usual talkative persona had been lacking over the past few days. I suspected this was heralding his declining physical condition: he didn't appear to be ill, just tired. In hindsight however, I should have been aware that he had something very private on his mind.

38

———————

I t was soon dark after leaving Wang, and Rocky slept soundly all the way to Albury. Nothing could be seen of the surrounding countryside through the dusty, glazed windows, other than the occasional pin prick of light emanating from a homestead in the near distance.

The train change at Albury went smoothly, entirely due to our ever patient, cooperative walers.

And even though it was past the normal scheduled time for dinner, the meal presented to us there, was first class country fare; roast lamb with gravy, mint gel and baked potatoes. There was even a delicious bowl of stewed apricots and clotted cream and as many cups of tea as we wanted.

The train service onto Sydney, was marginally more comfortable, but otherwise boring. That's not to say we didn't enjoy the country-side we passed through.

None of us had ever travelled to, let alone beyond Sydney Town. The stopover was routine, orderly and Rocky was able to stretch his legs and visit the toilet unassisted.

Our horses were, I think, glad to see me. They had plenty of feed and water and were able to move freely about their carriage.

However, they became a tad agitated when realisation struck that they were not about to be off loaded.

I was calming and, I hoped, reassuringly chatting to them, rubbing their ears and patting them in turn, when a voice intruded. 'They're pissed off I'd say. Need a bit of work, or a good walk.'

I spun around, surprised. In the gloom, there stood an attractive woman, in her mid-fifties I guessed. She was smiling broadly, albeit in a friendly manner and was dressed tidily in traditional farming garb, hair pulled back in a ponytail and her hat also hanging down her back.

'Oh, g'day there,' I said sheepishly, 'you gave me a bit of a fright.'

'Sorry; my name's Kay, no "e".'

'Leon,' I replied. 'Nice to meet you, Kay. You're right, these poor buggers have been on their feet for hours.'

'Look, Leon, this train won't be leaving for at least another half hour, so let's take 'em for a walk. There's a park about a hundred yards from here and there's no rules stopping us. So come on, we'll take three each; just follow me, I've done this a few times before, when I had my own horses ... before me husband got killed by a young bull a few years ago.'

I liked Kay immediately: she was just getting things done, not being pushy nor a smart arse, just happy to be able to help ... and perhaps just a bit lonely.

Despite the late time of night, we talked freely, even when we jogged with the horses, and we were partially out of breath.

I suspect it was not exactly what the horses needed but made good use of that half hour. By the time we got them back to the train, it felt like I had known Kay for many years.

Back at the station, we were met by Rocky and Dan ... and a local police officer.

Not surprisingly Rocky was obviously relieved to see me, but launched into what was probably a well-rehearsed, and well-deserved tirade.

'Bloody hell Leon, how many times do I ... '

Before he could really get going, Kay handed me the reins for the three horses she'd been exercising, and immediately then strode up to, and into Rocky's face.

'My name's Kay. Would you please desist, sir. I'm to blame for the disappearance of your horses; and Leon. Your horses needed to stretch their legs ... and I've done this several times before with my own horses.

'Sorry if I've upset you, or you, constable Emmerson; there's just been a simple misunderstanding.'

'Yes, I can see that, Mrs Bridges,' the policeman said politely, then added. 'So, there will be no charges. Better to be safe than sorry, I always say. And you've saved me a stack of paperwork. So, goodbye all ... and hopefully we can catch up on your way back to Wangaratta, eh Dan? You'll know where to find me.'

Kay helped me load and resettle the horses, but when we emerged from their carriage, Rocky was still standing there; still "gawping" is how I would best describe his appearance.

'By the way, Rocky,' I teased, 'Kay's also headed for Newcastle, and she'd love to travel with us. That OK with you Rocky?'

'Yeah, yes, of course; you are most welcome to join us Mrs. Bridges.

'Fair go, Rocky, please just call me, Kay.'

* * *

It was now approaching dawn and cool enough for fog to have settled over the station, and the train tracks disappeared in both directions into the fog.

Our seating arrangements differed slightly; Kay having insisted upon sitting next to Rocky!

Regardless, those notoriously uncomfortable train seats would soon make her backside ache as much as Dan's and mine already did. As for Rocky, I suspect he was oblivious to any discomfort, he had other far more important matters on his mind.

It escaped neither Dan's nor my observations that Rocky had come alive, and that Kay was happily reciprocating his complete and undivided attention. Moreover, no more than half an hour after leaving Sydney Town, Kay's head was resting on Rocky's shoulder, and she was sound asleep. Nice shot Cupid.

In that moment I yearned for Fay's company.

* * *

I HAVE to say that Dan and I were enthralled by the vastness and beauty of the surrounding fertile grazing and bush lands which seemed never ending, wherever, or whenever, one looked over the landscape.

By mid-morning the sun's searing heat had disposed of any lingering mist which had sought refuge in gullies and dry creek beds.

'It looks like being a scorcher, eh Leon?' Dan casually offered his thoughts, then added, 'there's a bloody lot of stock out there and I haven't seen any surface water for miles and miles.

'There's not that much shade either. Very different to the country around Warrnambool from where I come.'

'Or from Northeast Victoria, either,' I agreed. 'Anyway, I recently read somewhere that the Merino sheep which the early settlers brought with them originated in Spain, where it's a lot like this. I'm sure the farmers from around here must know a thing or two about what they're doin' by now.'

On impulse and without asking the other travelers their preference, Dan suddenly rose from his seat and manhandled three carriage windows half open, then propped wide open, two side doors: far better than turning into a grease spot just sitting there in stifling, stagnant heat. Well done Dan!

Soon, blue-grey humps of The Great Dividing Range rose in the east, stark against an azure, cloudless sky. Thankfully, a north easterly breeze was at work, bringing with it the unique fragrances of eucalyptus and freshly mown hay, which washed over our faces and delighted our senses.

39

Newcastle eventually exposed itself. Though located close to the ocean, on that day, there was not a hint of an offshore breeze to purge this town of the persistent stench of overcrowded humanity.

Our train journey now at an end, we led our fully laden horses from the station.

Kay, being a local, guided us to a nearby hotel which not only provided decent lodgings for some very weary travellers, but also had reasonable agistment for our horses.

In hindsight, it was not only a gallant gesture by Rocky to escort Kay to her small farm, but a reward for doing so, obviously earned him more than a kiss on the cheek: I didn't see him again until noon the next day.

His spirit was bubbling over in step with his observations of how wonderful the weather was, and how much he enjoyed listening to the seagulls and the rumble of not-too-distant surf.

* * *

IT TRANSPIRED, soon after having enjoyed a hearty midday meal and a reasonably cold pint of beer, that we met four cattlemen who looked the worse for wear.

'A big night on the grog, mate?' I enquired politely, yet hoping I sounded sympathetic.

'Nah, not really,' Ronald, the tallest and oldest chap replied, then added. 'We'd only had a few when five imbeciles started big noting 'emselves and doing a bit of pushin' and shovin' with our young Barry here. Bastards then went too far and knocked Barry's pint out of his hand ... accidental, on purpose like.'

'So, what happened then?' Dan asked in his usual, casual manner ... inviting further conversation given that he was not in police uniform.

'Well, an all-in soon got underway,' said Ronald, rubbing at his bruised chin. 'But the bloody coppers obviously got wind of what we were up to and arrived just as I reckoned we'd finally got the upper hand.

'Anyway, the cops waded into us with their truncheons, one and all, and no favourites, like. They were pretty good with them sticks I can tell you, so we called our little argument a draw.

'No arrests, just a good talking to from the cops ... and then we went our separate ways. A few blood noses and some nasty bruises was the only damage.'

'Things are all OK now I suppose, so let me buy you all a pint and let's relax like,' said Dan, now certain, he later confessed to me, that these blokes would turn out to be a gold mine of local information. And he was right.

When Dan shouted and tabled the third round of drinks, he quietly asked our new friend, Ronald, 'Do you know those blokes, or were they just out of town troublemakers?'

'The latter, matey. They come down from Dorrigo, every other week like. That Mickey bloke always seems ta 'av a chip on his shoulder. Incites trouble everywhere he goes. We should ah known betta and kept to ourselves.'

'So, that bastard lives in Dorrigo?' Dan asked feigning sympathy. 'We'd better give it a wide berth, eh?'

'It ain't actually a town. An' it's some distance away. Up in the mountains... somewhere in the old cedar cuttin' area. Most people hate Mickey's guts and there's no way he can be trusted. So yeah, I'd stay away from Dorrigo, if I were you.'

When Ronald was engaged in conversation with Rocky, Dan glanced in my direction and winked: a wink that said, 'too easy, his days are numbered now, eh.'

* * *

IT WAS undeniable Kay and Rocky had taken a genuine shine to each other, so much so it wasn't surprising when Rocky announced that Kay would be joining us on our quest.

'Why not?' said Kay. 'My late husband and I travelled to Dorrigo a few times with our horses to explore the beautiful country up that way, so I know a few shortcuts, and besides, you might appreciate my cooking.

'It'll still take us at least four days to get there, and you never know when you might need an extra shooter... and besides, I'm a bloody good shot with my faithful rifle if I may say so myself.

'I know you're wondering what Rocky's told the two of you about me, but he only revealed your intentions after I told him about my previous occupation.'

'Which was?' Dan interrupted.

'I was a cop: a senior investigator, mostly stationed in Newcastle.'

'Thought as much,' replied Dan. 'So am I, but I'm on secondment from Warrnambool, in Victoria's east. But that's another story. The bloke we're gunna nail is from Victoria, but I have authority for his official arrest—and if he stays alive, I'll be responsible for his legal transportation back to Victoria.'

'No problems with me, Dan. I'm now just a peaceful, law-abiding citizen; what you do with that bloke is your call. And whatever my replacement thinks about jurisdiction, we'll just do whatever needs to be done, and never tell him anything.'

'That'll do me Kay; welcome aboard.'

'So, Kay, since you're familiar with Dorrigo,' I asked, 'what's it like?'

'It's quite a small settlement on what's called the Waterfall Way … and it's at quite an altitude,' Kay reflected. 'Officially, Dorrigo resides in what's called the Northern Tablelands.

'I'm hoping that one day the area around Dorrigo will become a protected heritage park, or something like that. It really is a beautiful part of the world. The views are sensational, there's no shortage of waterfalls in a range of forest environments, plus there's an enormous variety of animals and birds.

'The only drawback is that the weather can be a bit fickle, and it can start snowing without much warning.'

Kay paused for a breath, then pressed on. 'Dorrigo also has a bit of a shady history, which unfortunately persists today.

'Cedar is still harvested in some of the more remote locations—primarily for boatbuilding I believe—but it really must stop before it's all gone.

'And … it still attracts an unhealthy criminal element.'

40

————

From memory, we spent the next three days recovering from our lengthy train trip. Dan and I basically became onlookers, Rocky however, hobbled about assisting Kay with her preparations.

A string of eight laden horses was not an uncommon sight, yet we chose to leave Newcastle well before daybreak. Kay, true to her word, nevertheless kept us away from major roads.

Our target may well have taken the same trails as us, and the probability was that he could have arrived in Dorrigo many months previously.

The journey from Newcastle was pleasant, the scenery fantastic as Kay had promised, the horses worked well together, and they were never short of fresh pickings and water. And Kay's cooking was far better than anything I'd previously tasted when either out mustering or trying to locate bad bastards.

However, towards the end of day three, despite the mountain air being cool and invigorating, we were suddenly made very aware that something nearby had died. As we rode into a small clearing, the smell was almost overpowering.

'Dead wallaby would be my guess,' I said, 'we're definitely not stopping here.'

'Nope, you're wrong this time Leon,' Dan quickly responded. 'I know that smell; you never forget it. Someone died here not that long ago.'

'With a bit of luck it was Mickey,' I said, more to myself than to anyone else.

'Unfortunately, it's my job to check this out,' Dan said as he dismounted. 'I suggest you all move on; you'll soon be downwind. I'll catch up with you soon enough. Go on! Shove off.'

Nobody protested; even the horses seemed distracted and needed no encouragement to keep moving.

True to his word, Dan caught up with us about half an hour later, at an idyllic location bordering a small, swiftly flowing, gin clear creek. The horses were browsing contentedly, and Kay and I were in the process of preparing our dinner. Rocky too, had wasted no time in getting a fire going and was happily plying it with some large, dry branches, which may well have been cedar.

I was not only glad to welcome Dan into our camp site, but my curiosity definitely needed satisfying. He dismounted, released his horse to join the others then strode over to the fire ... and had our complete and total attention.

'Well son, what yah got for us?' Rocky asked as he handed Dan a mug of freshly brewed tea.

'It was a bloke,' Dan began, then soldiered on. 'Maybe mid-forties, ginger hair—what was left of it—a full ginger beard and he was probably about six feet tall. He had no gun, or any identification; not even a wallet.'

'And?' Rocky encouraged Dan to continue.

'He was lying on his side, one arm sort of tucked under his body. He'd been shot twice; once in the back of his head, and once in the back.'

'Anything else?' Rocky asked.

'I made no attempt to bury him; someone else can do that, providing there's anything left of him once nature has its way.

'However, he was holding this, Rocky. Found it when I rolled him onto his back. Dunno how the killer missed it though ... it's quite a nice watch, eh?

'My guess is the shooter panicked or was in a hurry to catch that bloke's horse before it headed back into Dorrigo: all the sign indicates that anyway. So, whoever committed this murder is also up for horse theft.'

Rocky and I were gawping at each other, having simultaneously recognised the watch's significance, it being identical to the one I was wearing... the one previously owned by Adam, and which, to this very day I still wear with great pride.

'This watch is evidence Rocky, so I'll have to take responsibility for it,' said Dan. Without any objection, Rocky dutifully returned it to him.

I'm certain Dan missed the earlier look which passed between Rocky and me, but on the other hand, I was equally confident Kay had noticed, though she showed no sign she had done so.

As Kay and I completed preparing our meal, Rocky, as if in a trance, sat upwind of the fire, staring into it, occasionally prodding at the embers nearest to him.

Dan, on the other hand, had stripped down to his under garments and immersed himself and his outer clothes in the creek. He then proceeded to vigorously sluice water over his head and body, intending no doubt to rid himself of any lingering stench of putre-fying human flesh. Next, he thrashed his clothes around in the water, then rinsed and squeeze dried them multiple times.

Finally, he hung his wet clothes over an assortment of low hanging branches, downwind of the fire and declaring, 'I'd much rather smell of eucalypt smoke thanks very much.'

When Dan, having changed into dry clothes returned to the fire, Kay and I passed around dinner plates laden with our offering of damper, sausage, scrambled eggs and cheese.

Rocky hadn't been totally distracted because no sooner had we commenced eating than he made himself busy expertly pouring each of us a fresh brew of tea then passed our mugs around.

We ate in silence and when finished, enjoyed some barley sugar with a second mug of tea. However, an air of expectancy lingered; a silent void screamed to be filled.

'I've got something very personal to say,' Rocky said quietly, 'in fact, something I've only ever told to one other person, and that was Adam.

Realizing he had our undivided attention, Rocky pressed on. 'Probably, like the rest of you, it's my belief that chap we found back there was Mickey's handy work. It's now up to you, Dan, to gather whatever evidence exists to have him convicted of murder; clearly his death wasn't a case of suicide.'

'Keep going Rocky, darling,' Kay said quietly, 'get whatever it is off your chest.'

Physically gathering himself, Rocky took a deep breath and announced, somewhat tentatively. 'It so happens that Mickey is my bastard son. Never knew his mother, nor would it have done him any good, she lost her marbles not long after giving birth to him and ended up in a lunatic asylum. Been gone now for thirty-five or so years; perhaps more like forty years.

'Anyway, to my never to be forgotten disgrace I basically dumped him, and he became a Ward of the State. I had no contact with him whatsoever after that, until fifteen years later he somehow tracked me down. I never denied that I was his father and offered a roof over his head so long as he pulled his weight around the homestead and property.

'He was always a surly sod, that's for sure. He resented doing any job I gave him, which resulted in us arguing over many stupid little things ... and that eventually ended in fisticuffs. Yes, fisticuffs.

'Regardless, one day he took himself into Wang, got into cahoots with some local smart-arse, petty criminal types and soon moved out without so much as a wave goodbye. He never returned to the homestead unless he was desperate for money. Which, like a fool, I felt somewhat compelled to give him.

'Mickey despised Adam who had come to live on my property.' But that's a story for another day. I suspect Mickey was jealous of

Adam, though he had no need to feel like that: perhaps it was because Adam was younger than Mickey, and that I lavished too much attention on him, or, that Adam was aboriginal.'

'Give yourself a breather Rocky,' Kay suggested. 'Let's stop for another brew, and some fruitcake. '

'Yeah, let's,' replied Rocky, but quickly added. 'Just a few more things I need to spill.

'Even in his mid-teens, Mickey was blessed with the physique of a man which he used to influence his will on others. In hindsight, he obviously didn't make too many sensible decisions and soon found himself upsetting the police; and nothing seems to have ever changed.

'For example, as we know, during one of our mustering trips, Mickey even tried to shoot Adam, but luckily one of Adam's mob intervened.

'Anyway, back to the watch. When Adam's twenty first birthday was approaching, unbeknown to him, I visited Wang and purchased two identical watches, one for Adam and one for Mickey ... as his belated twenty first birthday gift.

'I had the shop keeper etch the letter "A" on the back of one watch, and "M" on the other. Go on Leon, look on the back of your watch case. What does it have?'

'I don't have to,' I said, 'I know there's a capital letter "A" scratched on it.'

'And now, Dan, what's on the back of the watch you retrieved?' Rocky asked.

'Well, I'll be buggered. There's an unmistakable capital "M" scratched on it.'

'And that sort of evidence should do the trick in any court of law,' Kay said confidently. 'But listen, let's leave things there for the moment. But Dan, I'd be happy to help you record and witness this little conversation as an official record of interview.'

41

———————

Upon arriving in Dorrigo, Kay took over just in time for the clouds were gathering and looking more and more black and menacing by the minute. She quickly led us through, and then a short distance beyond the settlement, where she suddenly stopped at a closed roadside gate. 'Here Leon, look smart,' she said, 'grab this key and open the padlock, there's a good lad.'

I dismounted, opened the padlock and walked the gate open. Kay had taken the reins of my horse and led it, and the rest of our mob into the fenced paddock which beckoned. Once everyone was through, Kay circled back and handed the reins back to me.

'Shut the gate please Leon. Loop the padlock through the chain but don't close it. Yeah, that's it, make it look as if it hasn't been disturbed, then follow me.'

The homestead, a well preserved, off-white colonial style building with wrap around verandas was set back from the road by at least two hundred yards, but there was no welcoming party; not even a dog.

For no other reason other than to familiarize myself, I turned in my saddle and looked back towards the town centre and was struck by the clear line of sight it possessed, not just along the main street, but for hundreds of yards in every other direction around the town.

'Right, everyone please dismount, and lead your horse in here,' Kay ordered cheerfully, 'that's if I can get these bloody doors open.'

I dismounted, and Kay said, almost as if talking to herself, 'I'm pretty sure that key you've got Leon also fits the shed padlock.' It did; and a minute later both shed doors were wide open, and all our horses were inside.

'So, who lives here Kay?' Rocky asked innocently.

'As luck would have it darling, it serves a few purposes. It becomes the residence for any visiting coppers and their families, and secondly, it acts as a lockup, but only has two cells. The last officer who lived here retired not that long ago, and the powers that are, haven't yet found a suitable replacement and understandably no one has volunteered for this placement. So, there yah go Dan, this place is officially yours until our job here is done.

'Anyway, that's enough gas bagging, let's get the horses unloaded and move our stuff inside. There's one main, and five single bedrooms, but only one long-drop and that's out the back.

'That door over there, opens onto a stairwell which leads up into the kitchen, but there's ample room to get your gear upstairs without getting hung up. But step on it, I ... '

As if to underscore Kay's suggestion for more haste, the sky was suddenly lit by multiple strikes of fork lightening and a simultaneous series of thunder claps so loud the house shook.

It would be fair to say that I jumped and damn nearly peed myself.

Our steadfast walers were also all put to the test, but soon recovered their equanimity after some snorting, hoof stamping and irritable head shaking.

Rocky and Dan had instantly stopped what they were doing and stood rigid and motionless. I remember hearing a stifled, unfinished expletive from Rocky, but Dan, would you believe, had turned a sort of greyish colour.

Later, though it had not stopped raining and thunder still boomed and echoed through the surrounding valleys, Kay and I opened the shed doors just in case the walers felt adventurous; they weren't, even though the police paddock at the back of the house had a lush pick.

42

It didn't stop raining for the next three days, though "rain" was hardly the right word to describe the deluge which soaked Dorrigo and the surrounding mountains. How, I wondered, could clouds hold so much goddamn water?

First there was significant sheets of runoff, then new streams were born and at day two, most of the surrounding gullies were in flood which wrought havoc upon out-buildings and post-and-rail fences.

The police station being elevated, survived quite well, except for a few leaks from the veranda.

The long drop however, had to fight gamely to stay upright and serviceable.

* * *

By DAY FOUR, food was running very low. A trip into town was planned, but we agreed Rocky should remain at home with Kay. Several people knew Kay from her previous life as Dorrigo's resident policewoman, or when she returned as a civilian with her late husband and would readily recognise her ... which was exactly what we didn't want. Surprise, after all, would serve our agenda well.

Even a bearded white man walking the main street in the company of a black man would not raise as much talk about town, as would those people who'd recognise me,' Kay insisted pragmatically.

So, off into Dorrigo, Dan and I went, armed with a shopping list. Most recognised us as strangers, no doubt, but none failed to acknowledge us as just passing through. Most seemed happy for a casual chat about the dreadful weather, the terrible flooding, how their stock would handle such wet conditions, or when they could leave town to count and attend their stock.

It wasn't long after we had successfully completed our shopping, that we got the information we so desperately needed.

As Dan and I gazed across the expansive flood waters, two old folks approached us. The old lady, full of concern and wanting to chat, finally said, 'Yah knows, I feel really sorry for them who live up in them mountains like. It won't be easy for them timber workers and station workers tah get into town tah get supplies; they might perish up there yah knows.'

Quick as a flash, albeit sounding as if he really did give a damn, Dan asked, 'so how on earth do you reckon they can get back to Dorrigo safely, like?'

'Some have hand-me-down wooden row boats,' the old bloke volunteered, 'but how safe they'd be I can't say. Mind you, if I had to choose between starving to death and drowning, I reckon I'd give an old rowboat a chance.'

'Would they land their boats here, or somewhere else before heading into town?' I asked, more so to keep the conversation going than to seek more information.

'I don't reckon they'd be stupid enough to attempt a return trip in their boat while carrying provisions; not while this flood's still up.'

'I don't really care young fella,' said the old bloke. 'They knew the risks of livin' up there. This water's gunna hang around for months now, so my guess is they'll head for the coast; probably start new lives … who cares?'

While walking back to the borrowed police station, Dan suddenly stopped and placed a hand on my forearm. 'Hang on a bit Leon. Look, up there, what can you see?'

'That's a wedge tailed eagle, for sure. Looking for a mate perhaps?'

'Nah, he's looking for me. He wants to tell me something; about Mickey I do believe.

'The wedge tail eagle is known as *Bunjil*; creator of all back people and my totem creature. We share our thoughts and must always protect each other.

'Don't be offended Leon but please give me ten minutes alone. I'll catch up with you back at the homestead soon enough.'

* * *

ROCKY AND KAY greeted me as I walked up the path to the homestead.

'Where's Dan?' Rocky asked, his voice tinged with concern.

'He's OK. He should be back here shortly, and I suspect he'll have some news. Let me offload this shopping and I'll fill you in.'

No sooner had I rejoined Rocky and Kay on the front veranda, than Kay said, 'Here comes Dan now, and he's in a bit of a hurry by the look of him.'

Dan, puffing slightly, paused at the top step, turned and pointed skyward. 'There! That's Mickey's undoing,' he said excitedly.

It only took a few seconds to spot the eagle slowly drifting high above the town. Abruptly, though faint, we heard several long-drawn-out screeches typical of a wedge tail eagle when hunting.

'Don't ask me to explain now, but we must move quick smart if we want to nail Mickey; right now, he's heading for Dorrigo. Leon and I should be able to make the arrest, so Kay, you and Rocky don't need to attend.'

'And miss all the fun?' Be buggered. No way,' Kay replied.

Dan and I, now both armed and with one already up the spout, set a good pace back into town. Rocky however, visibly hindered by his chronic leg and back pain was unable to keep up. Kay, ever attentive, slowed to his pace and put a supporting arm around his midriff.

Dan led us to the location where earlier, we gazed over the flooded valley and talked with the old couple. 'There!' said Dan excitedly, pointing to the mid-distance. 'That's him, roughly level with that little promontory on the western bank.'

'Come on Dan, how can you tell it's him? His back's facing us, in the normal rowing position. Mind you, whoever it is, he's making reasonable progress.'

'Believe me Leon, if it wasn't him, that wedge tail wouldn't be circling overhead. Play along with me Leon. Let's get out of sight and see what unfolds.'

We retreated to a small picnic pavilion, which fortuitously, provided an unhindered view of the flood's foreshore, to where the rower seemed intent upon heading.

When the rower was about twenty yards from the bank, he glanced over his shoulder to no doubt decide upon his exact landing place. And that was when we made a fundamental mistake, electing to prematurely reveal our hiding position.

Almost immediately the rower took an unanticipated second glance and immediately saw the two of us approaching him, our firearms drawn and levelled at him.

The rower immediately sensed his precarious situation and, in a split second, desperately set about trying to manoeuvre his boat away from the bank, believing no doubt that his distance, and the likely inaccuracy of our handguns over that distance would save his neck.

What we didn't expect was, as soon as he had rowed another twenty or so yards further away from the bank, that he would produce a rifle and aim it in our direction.

Despite the facts that the boat was unstable resulting from his exertions to retrieve his rifle, and that the distance between us had increased twofold, that rifle was now pointing directly at me, rock steady and very life threatening.

Two things then happened for which I will forever remain grateful.

In a flurry of large flapping wings, talons and high-pitched screeching, out of the blue an eagle struck the would-be shooter.

That attack made him scramble for cover while waving the barrel of his rifle over and around his head. I have to say, he was somewhat lucky for he successfully struck the eagle, forcing it to fall, injured and obviously in pain, into the flood water.

In the meantime, Dan and I were still in the open, and only just in retreat as the rower rebalanced his position and again took aim at me, though in hindsight, it might have been Dan who became his target; we'll never know.

Abruptly, there was a loud bang, followed almost immediately by a second round. Had it not been for Adam's advice about two years previously, I would not have thrown myself onto the ground and rolled. But I did ... and luckily, I found some cover provided by a small thicket of nearby scrub.

I risked a quick glance towards the boat, and then in the direction from where I reckoned those two shots had come. Not ten yards to my right stood Kay balancing herself to deliver a third shot.

Out on the flood water, the rower had abandoned his rifle for his paddle and was again frantically trying to increase the distance between himself and the shore.

'Kay! No!' I shouted as loud as I could. 'We need him alive.'

'Leon, if I wanted him dead, he'd be long gone,' she replied calmly. 'I'm not shooting at him; I'm aiming at his goddamn boat ... as near as I can get to the waterline. He'll soon have to make up his mind about his next move.'

We watched as Kay fired a fourth and fifth round in quick succession, enjoying the obvious discomfort now confronting the boat's master as his vessel suddenly listed to port and began sinking rather quickly.

No doubt resigned to his dilemma; the bloke hostilely abandoned his boat and struck out for shore. Dan was quickly in position to welcome him and wasted no time snapping his handcuffs shut around the man's wrists as he stepped onto dry land.

'Well, well, well,' Dan chimed, 'if it isn't just the bloke we want to question.

'Welcome to Dorrigo Mickey, but you're well and truly under arrest on multiple counts which I'll serve upon you shortly enough.'

'Who the hell are you, yah black bastard? And who gives that bitch the right to shoot at someone who's unarmed and can't protect himself?'

'You're being delusional as always,' I said. 'Your numbers up Mickey, and you'll be going away for a long time. And this gentleman is Senior Constable Cameron of the Victorian Police Force.'

'Ah, I didn't recognise you at first, but you're that smart-arse kid who works for that old bastard Rocky. I shoulda killed yah while I had the chance.'

'And thank you, sir, for that comment,' said Kay in strict parlance, 'which will be used in evidence, with me as witness ... for attempted murder. So, Dan, include that remark when you write up this idiot's charges.'

As Dan started to frog-march Mickey away, Rocky abruptly stepped in front of Mickey and said,' Yah knows what son? I may be getting old, but it's you who'll always be a bastard ... and a no bloody good one at that.'

* * *

'By the way, Dan,' I said later, 'did you notice that the eagle made its way back to shore? Probably saved me life!'

'Yes, I did, thanks Leon. And do you know what? I sense you just might now believe in blackfella magic.'

43

———

Mickey was locked in a cell at the homestead come police station, but not before introducing him to the joys of joined ankle restraints. The only concessions he received was a dry pair of prisoner overalls and a second blanket.

'It seems a waste to feed this rotter,' I pondered with Dan. 'Surely he's gunna swing before too long.'

'He's not doing himself any favours either,' Dan added. 'He flat out refuses to confess anything or show any remorse and persists in throwing unsavoury threats at Kay. Perhaps his only defence might be that he gets judged to be deranged, but either way, he's not long for this world.

'You know Rocky much better than me, Leon. What effect is Mickey's arrest having upon him?'

'Perhaps twelve months ago he may have protected Mickey, as if he still had some parental responsibility for his behaviour. But not now; I think this murder has been the last straw, seeing what he can do and not care a tinker's toss.

'I also think meeting Kay has done wonders for Rocky. I'm sure she must have got stuck into him and opened his eyes to the possibilities of a decent life after Mickey.

'I hope Rocky can convince Kay to come and live with all of us on his property. I'm sure Fay and Elspeth, and Max of course, will make her feel at home. I know I will; she's a God send.'

'What about you Dan? Do you reckon you'll take on Don Carmichael's job? I know he likes how you go about things and will support you one hundred percent if you accept.'

'Depends on a couple of things Leon. I know my wife and kids will support me, no matter what. I'll insist on receiving an automobile; that's the way of the future. And I'll do everything in my power to eliminate segregation of black kids from white kids, particularly in school or on the playing field.'

'That can be accommodated, surely. But there might be a few hiccups along the way, particularly given some of the stupid racial issues cropping up in the big cities.'

'So, is that all you need to get you to relocate to Wang?'

'Yep, except for one other thing.'

'Which is?'

Looking straight into my eyes, Dan said quietly. 'I'll take the job on, but only if *you* work with me. I don't mean *for* me Leon, I mean, *with* me.'

'I'm with you my friend, but let's wait and see how Fay feels about being a coppers' wife.'

We then shook hands; our unwritten pledge given in trust as strong and as enduring as steel.

44

It was now time to return Mickey to Wangaratta.

Since his arrest three days earlier, the rain had been replaced by warm, balmy conditions including a gentle breeze slightly tainted by the ocean's ozone, albeit the ocean was forty or so miles away.

The flood waters were receding and there was an air of impatience to get underway, besides our prisoner was as moody as he was foul mouthed ... and moreover, a tiresome responsibility.

Rocky and Kay went into town and purchased an ageing horse and bridle, both very obviously qualifying as second-hand: both part of Dan's plan to minimise any attempt by Mickey to escape along the way. No consideration was given to providing him with a saddle, further, no doubt, dissuading Mickey from contemplating a break away.

Worse for Mickey, his ankle cuffs were replaced with handcuffs which were firmly tethered to a special "arrest belt" around his midriff, an ungainly piece of equipment which could only be released by somebody else, from behind his back.

Mickey would be able to use his hands, and he would no doubt have been able to control his horse. However, depending upon how he behaved, or misbehaved, even that small privilege would then be denied to him; his horse would then be led by halter secured to the rear of the saddle of the rider preceding him.

Toilet stops would prove to be frustrating and time wasting because Mickey had to be assisted with dismounting and remounting. If he caused any trouble whatsoever, or failed to properly attend to his ablutions, he would soon find himself walking for the next mile or two, tethered by rope behind his horse.

Most of the return trip to Newcastle was uneventful, except in the afternoon of the third day. As we rounded a bend in the track where tall eucalyptus abounded on both sides, we suddenly came upon five riders, in single file. As protocol dictates, I led our string to the left-hand side of the track and called for a stop, for no other reason than to get the lowdown on the tracks condition ahead of us.

The other blokes stopped their horses, but acted uncomfortably, as if they were hatching something nefarious. Very quickly however, their demeanours altered when they identified Mickey and his hapless circumstances.

'Have a look at who we have here boys!' shouted the leading rider. 'None other than that no good, cheatin', lyin' and thiev'n bastard, Mickey.'

Another rider taunted. 'Off to a party eh Mickey? A necktie party I'd say.'

A third rider added. 'Make sure someone relieves him of the ten quid he still owes me.'

Another added mercilessly, 'Yah shiverin there Mickey, but it's such a lovely warm day. Pity yah won't be seein' too many more yah miserable bastard.'

'OK, lads, that'll be enough Tom Foolery for now,' I said calmly, but quickly continued. 'Are you all heading for Dorrigo?'

'What's it to yah,' the lead rider replied belligerently.

'Can't have you misbehaving and upsetting the good folk of Dorrigo.'

'If yah must know, we're going to help a bloke do some musterin'. After all that rain, they'll probably be all over the place, like.'

'Could be slippery work,' I said, trying not to sound too facetious if they got my drift. 'Please ensure you also rescue any cleanskins you run into. As I said, we can't have you upsetting the locals, can we? You really don't wanna end up like this unhappy sod do yah?

'Cheerio boys.'

With that said, both parties went their own way.

Mickey, poor bugger, sat hunched over and looked totally miserable; seemingly not hearing the ribald comments left for him to contemplate as his uncaring friends filed past.

'Nicely handled Leon,' said Kay. 'You've given 'em something to think about, that's for sure.'

'I wonder how long it'll be before we hear about another gang of five young blokes commercialising cattle that aren't theirs?' Dan added pragmatically, albeit cynically.

'I'm not so sure,' answered Rocky, 'once those blokes realise that they're likely to become fair game, they surely won't risk being *legally* shot at by not only common bounty hunters, or by anyone else for that matter trying to earn a quid or two.'

* * *

THE REMAINING journey back to Newcastle was made faster and easier the closer we got to our destination, this section being made wider to cope with a greater and more frequent volume of local traffic.

It would be an understatement that my thoughts had been turning more and more to Fay and Charlotte. I wasn't morose, but often found myself guilty of being deeply immersed contemplating our future.

Again, as luck would have it, the hotel where we had previously stayed was again able to accommodate us and our horses; but on the other hand, wanted nothing to do with our traveling companion.

'I expected as much,' said Kay, 'but that's not unreasonable; I know exactly who'll be glad to see him and who'll take him off our hands for a few days.'

And so, Mickey was escorted to Newcastle's main police station and introduced to the duty Seargent, Jason Newey, who with little ceremony, frog marched Mickey to a cell. I was glad it was him, and not me, who was going to occupy that cell because it was even more restrictive than the deprivations that he had so far endured on the trail with us.

I'm sure, by the look of Mickey's gaunt, pallid face, that he was now very much regretting his earlier chosen lifestyle.

Seargent Newey slid the heavy-duty steel cell door shut with a solid clunk, then locked it with a well-practised turn of a huge key. 'That's how they all look Leon, once they know the games up. It's the total loss of freedom that gets to 'em.

'I've received reports about this bloke over several years, but I've never had the manpower to nail him. So, thanks folks, you've done me a favour even though I'd like more time to discuss his involvement in several matters other than murder.'

'Thanks Jason,' said Kay, 'we'll be back in three days to collect him. That'll give us time for a bit of rest and to organise our transport back to Wangaratta. But please, just one last favour ... please teach him how to use the sluice, he stinks.'

'It'll be a pleasure, Kay. But I know absolutely nothing about all this, right? So, please don't lodge anything formal, like; I don't need the bloody paperwork.'

* * *

FOR THE NEXT two days a persistent and strong north easterly wind battered the coastline and which, combined with successive high tides, created spectacular sets of huge waves and sent them charging up the beach, where they systematically demolished the sand dunes for as far north and south as you could see.

Fortunately, the wind backed off rapidly before those wave surges inundated nearby farming land, but nevertheless significant damage had been inflicted not only upon the town's waterfront infrastructure, but several small wooden boats were wrecked, and two ocean going ships had pulled their anchor chains and were now left grounded.

While Dan and I were surveying this carnage, we were joined by a group of local on-lookers.

'Both of those ships were fully laden and were scheduled to depart for Sydney, today,' an old, bearded chap said. 'No perishables, but they'll both have to be unloaded before the Harbour Master can authorize any attempt to refloat 'em'.

'Could you re-consign their loads somehow?' I asked, not intending to say what I was thinking.

'Not by sea, mate, that's for sure,' added the old bloke. 'It could be months before suitable ships can be found. And we won't have been the only port hit by this storm, so getting tugs up from Sydney may also take months. You know; first in, first served, will rule.'

'Plus, whoever's got the deepest pockets might have something to do with that,' I said, again hoping I wasn't stating the obvious.

'What about using local carriers; those who can put together horse and cart teams?' Dan suggested politely.

'Yeah, that'd work,' replied the old bloke. 'But that ain't up to me.

'Mind yah, this blow ain't the worst we've had. Over the years we've lost plenty of ships and seamen along this 'ere bit of coastline. Yah can see for yah selves, just 'alf a mile north from here. There're a few skeletons stuck fast there, and still breakin' up.'

'Same from where I come from,' Dan added.

'An' where would that be sonny boy?' the old boke replied.

'Warrnambool; on the west coast in Victoria.'

'Nah, never heard of it.' the old bloke muttered as he turned and walked away.

45

The following morning Kay and Rocky walked to the railway station to secure our tickets for the train journey back to Albury. The result: we had to be at the station by no later than five thirty to guarantee sufficient time for us to load our horses, and of course, not upset the New South Wales train timetable.

The only problem with that arrangement was how and when would we take delivery of Mickey. There was no way in the world Seargent Newey would agree to getting out of bed at such a god forsaken hour to prepare Mickey.

However, it was Kay to the rescue who talked the good sergeant into having Mickey "ready for the road" before retiring. Not only that, but Sergeant Newey handed Kay the keys to both the station and for Mickey's cell … on the proviso she promised to lock up and then leave both keys within the guard dog's kennel before departing with Mickey.

The best news of that day was Kay's decision to accompany Rocky back to his property. Though they had only known each other for a week or so, the first idea that popped into my mind was *"I bet they get married"*.

For most of that day we spent preparing ourselves and our horses for that journey to Albury. Fay was in no mood to "pack any stuff that she could probably purchase in Wangaratta", so it took her little time to assemble her few chosen belongings.

These activities also provided me with time to reflect upon my beautiful wife and daughter, whose company by now, I missed greatly. Yet it was Rocky who distracted me, inviting conversation with me about my plans.

His interest was genuine. His greatest fear being what would happen to the property if Fay agreed with me becoming a copper, and what would happen if I got killed in the line of duty: who'd take over?

However, from my perspective at that time, I was only looking forward to attending livestock auctions where I could buy quality bulls to start our own Hereford bloodline, and to start improving the overall quality of my cattle.

* * *

WE ALL MADE it to the train station on time, despite Mickey's ramblings and protestations, and our walers again behaved in their customary accepting nature as they were led into a dedicated, purpose-built horse carriage. Attendants had already filled their individual hay bins and water tubs.

'So, Mickey, you'll notice, I hope, that we'll be travelling First Class on this leg of our journey,' I said firmly, but quickly added, 'but if you speak out of turn, or in any way try to escape or disrupt us, or any of the others travelling with us, you'll be given two options.

'The first is that you'll be muzzled and not fed, and the second will see you muzzled then thrown in with that herd of pigs in the carriage behind us. I'm told that pigs piss and shit a lot and have been known to kill and eat humans. It's a long trip Mickey, so don't be an idiot; behave yourself.'

* * *

THE MANDATORY TRAIN change at Albury was executed with precision. New tickets were purchased, and our belongings transferred into a First-Class passenger carriage.

Before departure, somewhat rushed toilet breaks were taken, including for our well restrained felon. Whereafter, for his unexpected, good behaviour, was given a mug of tea and a couple of buttered scones.

However, we all soon learned that *First Class* in Victorian trains was a euphemism; that status meaning nothing more than a non-adjustable footrest and that perhaps an extra handful of straw had been added to the padding of our worn and stained leather covered seats.

The journey south was tedious, but it was impossible not to be impressed by the scenery: fertile plains, stands of eucalyptus trees, huge rivers, well-advanced crops of wheat and barley, and to the east, the ever present Great Dividing Range.

* * *

IT WAS APPROACHING nightfall when the train stopped at the Wangaratta Railway Station. Weary passengers, all no doubt keen to stretch their legs, were losing no time exiting the train, lugging their belongings with them. The air was cool, and the initial happy exchange of welcome and greetings between family and friends took only minutes to lessen as they exited the station.

'Right, let's get our horses off-loaded,' said Rocky. 'We all know the drill, and I know we're all a bit buggered, but the sooner we get moving the easier it should be. The fresh air'll do us all good, and it should only take another few hours to reach Leon's property.'

Rocky spoke those words as if the property had always been mine; I wasn't stunned, but I certainly felt an enormous rush of pride knowing that was in fact the truth. And I didn't miss the not-so-subtle nudge Dan delivered to my back as he walked by.

Surprisingly, Mickey seemed resigned to his fate and cooperated as Dan, and I heaved him onto his horse. 'Not long now, Mickey, and you can have these bracelets off,' Dan advised him. 'So don't spoil things by making any last-minute attempt to escape, or you just might die from a dose of lead poisoning.'

Upon our arrival at The Wangaratta Police Station, it was approaching nine o'clock at night. We were clearly not expected by the duty constable at this hour, but when the station Captain, our good friend Don Carmichael, was roused, the atmosphere became welcoming, for all but you know who.

After greetings all round, Rocky proudly introduced Kay, to Don. 'Can't talk now, we've got to get a move on if we wanna be home before breakfast. Give us a couple of weeks to get settled then call by with your wife. Make it for lunch on a Sunday; we've got heaps to fill you in on mate.'

'Yes, I can imagine you do. We'll be there. Nice meeting you Kay.'

Don then turned his attention to Mickey. 'Well, son, you seem to be in a spot of bother, much more than your poor bloody father ever wanted to see.'

'I'm not your goddam son, and this ain't entirely my fault!' Mickey snapped back. 'That old mongrel never gave me a second thought, and now it seems he's given up his entire property to this Johnny-come-lately, money grubbin', black lovin' turd.'

'That'll be enough of that language,' Don ordered, then added with equal venom. 'It's quite clear to me that I know your father and Leon much, much better than you do.'

And with that, Don firmly guided Mickey to a cell, nudged him inside and slammed the self-locking door shut with a thunderous *clang*.

46

Having farewelled Don, we pressed our horses eastward. They were up to it; not tripping or stumbling once in the reduced night light, while maintaining the fast, rhythmic walking pace for which they are so admired.

Regrettably, Rocky was tiring and a candidate to soon nod off, fall from his saddle, and inflict serious injury to himself. Kay again proved her worth, riding close beside Rocky's mount and every time Rocky sagged, she would give him a sharpish jab in his ribs. That routine worked long enough to get him home safely ... just.

However, though Rocky had become irritable with that treatment, he made no protest when Dan, Kay and I somehow managed to carry him, fast asleep, from his horse, up the front veranda steps and into his bedroom.

Unfortunately, we had unintentionally awakened Elspeth, Max and Fay. Thankfully, once Max realised who had intruded the house, and moreover interrupted their sleep, he graciously lowered his shotgun.

In a flash, Fay was in my arms, planting kisses all over my face, and I swear, she was purring as she matched the strength of my embrace. She suddenly broke free, grabbed my hand and tugged me into our old bedroom while whispering, 'ssshhhh.'

In the subdued light of the bedside lantern, there was Charlotte, sitting bolt upright in the bed, head cocked slightly to one side with curiosity, and smiling broadly as if she could hardly believe who it was with her mum. When she suddenly threw her arms wide apart and muttered "da", I gasped, but managed, 'Yes, 'tis me, our beautiful girl.'

'Well, go on, pick her up,' Fay said impatiently, 'but don't squeeze her as hard as when you just attacked me.'

I didn't realise tears were running down my face, so intense was the incredible love and joy I experienced in the moment that Charlotte reached for my face and touched those tears.

Refreshments were offered but declined, sleep was our priority.

Yet, as tired as Dan and I were, we unsaddled and unburdened the horses, roughly stacked the saddles, reins and our camping paraphernalia into the main shed, then pushed the horses out into the home paddock with a promise of a decent session with the curry comb sometime the next day.

When I finally staggered back to the homestead, it would have been silent inside, had Rocky not been snoring on top note. *Buggered if I know how Kay will cope with that?'* I thought.

Regardless, I snuck a look into Rocky's bedroom and there was Kay, snuggled up against Rocky and snoring gently in rhythm with her new lover. And that pleased me.

Despite my best intentions, Dan alone, attended to the horses the next morning.

47

Over the next two or three days, all of us except Charlotte, set about sorting, brushing and wiping clean everything which was splattered with mud, then aired our camping gear, making good use of the top rails of the yards adjacent to the shed in which we were working.

Max was in his element repairing or replacing frayed leather harness items.

When Dan had similarly attended to his own belongings, he then set himself up on the front veranda with two chairs and a small table and threw himself into completing his official police report.

Occasionally he would stop what he was doing and call out to Kay. 'I say, Kay, give me a hand with this would you please.' It was interesting to watch the two of them harmoniously at work; one the enthusiastic novice copper going places, and the other a retired Senior Sergeant.

'Just the facts Dan, nothing but the facts', I heard Kay say on several occasions.

When Kay was not alongside Dan, she and Fay took it upon themselves to wipe clean all the saddles and bridles and then apply to each item, a coat of leather preserving oil.

Elspeth and Fay plied us with tea, fruit cake, biscuits and toffee: indeed, one of us only had to glance in the direction of the house, that they'd bustle off to the kitchen.

But the best of all was when Fay brought Charlotte outside to supervise her father. Jeez, it was great being home.

During those days, though none of us worked like navvies, it became the norm for Rocky and Kay to retire inside for a mid-arvo nap. Yeah, well, I gave them the benefit of the doubt that that really was their intention.

On day four, Dan took his leave; his initial destination being Wangaratta so that he could 'talk turkey' with Don Carmichael about the job and timetable for him to replace Don.

Deep down, I felt everything would progress as Don wanted.

'I'll let you know how things pan out Leon, just as soon as I get home and discuss everything with me wife and kids,' said Dan casually, as we shook hands.

'Good luck mate,' I replied confident we were out of earshot from the others. 'By the way Dan, how old *are* your wife and kids?'

'Leah's about the same age as Fay, give or take a year or two. Our son, Archie's goin' on four, and Zoe's goin' on two. Why? I thought I'd told you that.'

'Yeah, yah did actually, it's just that Fay reckons she's pregnant again.'

Dan whacked a hand on his thigh, smiled broadly, knowingly. He then turned in his saddle, raised and waved his hat and called, 'Bye for now my friends; take care.'

The last thing I heard him say as he kicked his horse up into a canter was, 'you'll bloody well know you're alive now Leon.'

High overhead *Bunjil* soared, drifting lazily in the general direction of Wangaratta.

* * *

It only took Fay and Charlotte and me a few hours to move back into our cottage. Everything was spick and span, welcoming and comfortable. There were few jobs to do on the outside, the hallmark of Max's generous efforts.

'See what you've done to me again, you brute of a man,' said Fay as she lay beside me, gently rubbing her belly. 'You'll have to lift your game now boyo because I can't do everything. But you're forgiven, your son will be here in about seven months.'

'Our son,' I emphasised, somewhat surprised at her firm conviction of the child's gender. 'How, pray tell, can you possibly know it'll be a boy?'

'Anna Portesi, of course. She knows a thing or five about having kids. By the way, you can expect Frank to turn up any time soon; reckons his Durif needs a second opinion.'

In fact, the Portesi family turned up on the following Friday; Anna laden with her exotic Italian smallgoods and cake, and yes, Frank with two bottles of his favourite red wine. Their kids, always happy and helpful, spent most of their time, playing with Charlotte and drew great cheers when they eventually coaxed Charlotte to take her first few steps.

How lucky we were to have found such wonderful friends. Frank's wine disappeared rather quickly that afternoon, but he was also the bearer of some private, not so good, but not unexpected news.

'I say, Leon anda beautifulla Fay, it ah very sadah that your olda folks they struggle. Max, he fell arse ova the head a few weeksa go, anda I think he does not see too well these a days. He now wants hang on everything for balancing and he forget ta button his a trousers. An he piss himself. That a not good and he feel very embrass'd.'

Anna had placed her hand upon my arm, and when Frank paused for a breath, she said, 'I talk with a Fay and her mum abouta this, Leon. She also notta so well; gets dizzy and when she tries to talk she much troubled that her words sometimes getta mixed ... and a she forgets many things.'

For some time after Fay and I said goodbye to the Portesi family, we sat quietly debating what we now had to confront. This circumstance was occurring far sooner than either of us, and I daresay for Elspeth and Max, ever anticipated.

It was encouraging, yet sad, that Elspeth and Max, in a moment of common recognition of their plight, were able to agree and then tell us what they wanted, or rather, what they both needed.

With great courage I believe, Max asked for our help to find somewhere, preferably in Wang, for them to take up residence where they could receive care and not have to worry about buying food, preparing meals or general housework. 'We were hoping our son Bertie, would always be there for us,' Max said reasonably, 'but he's been a bit of a disappointment as you well know, Leon.

'And we'll miss Charlotte terribly,' Elspeth added before she started weeping.

The very next day, Fay and I, with Charlotte in tow, drove Rocky's buggy into Wang to search for a suitable place to take on Elspeth and Max.

Not only did Don Carmichael come with us to show us the way, but he introduced us to the owner of a small hospice, owned and operated by non-other than his sister, Janet, who also knew Rocky well, as her brother's best friend.

After a tour of the premises, Fay said quietly, 'Darling, this is absolutely perfect; no need to keep looking, eh?' The price was agreed, a formal contract signed, and a suitable deposit was gratefully handed over to Janet.

We shared morning tea with Don and Janet. Charlotte for some reason, took a shine to Don and spent most of the time sitting on his knee. Half an hour later, suitably refreshed, we thanked Don and Janet and were on the way back to our property.

It was during this trip that I handed the reins to Charlotte. With Fay's expert guidance she quickly overcame any fear, and soon our game little girl was flapping the reins on the horses back and trying to emulate Fay's mouth clicks to encourage the horse to go faster.

It had been a big day for Charlotte, and she eventually fell asleep in Fay's arms, with only a mile to go.

Three days later Fay and I transported Elspeth and Max into

Wang to appraise what we had unearthed for them. Elspeth was impressed; Max not so much initially, but after wandering alone inside the hospice and then in the peaceful lawned gardens outside, he eventually capitulated.

Halfway home, Max said with genuine feeling, 'I say, Leon, I think Elspeth and I should move into that lovely place right away; in fact, can we do so this coming weekend?'

48

In the two weeks prior to Don Carmichael and his wife Brenda arriving for Sunday lunch, Kay and Fay had preparations under control. Kay was in her element demonstrating her cooking prowess extended far beyond campsite cuisine, and on several occasions, in private, Fay spoke enthusiastically about Kay's amazing skills and patience, and how much she was learning from her.

Only one "kitchen accident" occurred during those preparations. Some biscuits which Fay was determined to cook on her own, somehow suddenly burst into smoke.

Bear in mind that my agreed duties that day were confined to rescuing them from a very curious Charlotte when they were busy. You decide whose fault it was that mayhem followed.

Both women were in the second verse of a ribald ditty which Kay had taught my not so innocent wife, when they both suddenly burst into laughter. Being curious about what had triggered that, and believing it would be OK, I allowed Charlotte to waddle on her own into the kitchen. Seeing her mother and Kay in such a happy state, she thought no doubt, that she should join in.

Her joyous attempt sent both women onto another level of laughter. My scurrying attempt to grab Charlotte from knocking something over and hurting herself, became another source of even greater hilarity, so much so that Kay had to rush outside to get some air before collapsing from loss of being able to breathe.

That's when disaster struck.

Fay's laughter suddenly changed to screaming, and our bewildered daughter followed suit. I quickly identified the reason because the kitchen was very quickly filling with black smoke. Grabbing the biscuit skillet by its handle, I dashed for the front door, but unintentionally knocked Kay onto her backside as she was returning inside to see what the hell had happened.

Suddenly realising how bloody hot the handle of the skillet was, I threw it away, not expecting the damn thing would strike the underside of the veranda and shower its contents over Kay.

Unbeknown to us, Rocky had just arrived at our cottage for a cuppa. The last thing the poor bugger would have been expecting to witness was me flattening Kay and then determinedly throwing black smoking offerings all over the love of his life.

* * *

Despite that event, the only unplanned change resulted from Fay's suggestion, and Rocky's insistence, that lunch be transferred to the homestead dining room; our cottage would be far too small to comfortably seat everyone.

Most unexpectedly, two bottles of Durif were found that morning in our roadside post box: compliments of the generosity of Frank Portesi.

The wine didn't last very long, both Don and Brenda quickly became avid fans and put just enough pressure on me to open the second bottle once they learnt that roast lamb was on the menu.

That lunch with Don and Brenda Carmichael was a resounding success and laced with fun. Kay, and her enthusiastic apprentice chef, otherwise known as Fay, together produced a superb three course meal.

However, biscuits didn't make it onto the menu.

It was reassuring Rocky could be with us for that meal and he wasted no time in asking for seconds. Don had not missed the cosy arm that Kay casually draped around Rocky's shoulder, nor the gentle kiss they shared.

'Well, well, well, Rocky,' Don exclaimed with great excitement. 'I don't know how you do it you ugly old bugger; you've always been a bit sneaky. Mind you Kay, he's the salt of the earth in my books, and you're a very lucky woman to have snared him. Congratulations, both of you.'

Kay smiled proudly.

Rocky methodically scooped another spoonful of stewed nectarines into his mouth, then winked in appreciation at Don.

* * *

FOLLOWING LUNCH, we all retired to the front veranda.

'I've got some news that might interest everyone,' Don announced. 'First, I reckon you'll be as proud as I am ... and relieved. 'Dan and I had an in-depth talk about his future before he headed back to Warrnambool. Since then, I've received his signed formal Offer of Employment, which now only requires the Victorian Chief Commissioner of Police's signature, who I just happen to know quite well. So, Dan should arrive back in Wang in about a fortnight to take up his job.'

I'm sure I cheered loudest, though Rocky wasn't far behind. Everyone clapped and whah hooed for this was a moment in history, as it should have been played out over a hundred years earlier. While shaking Don's hand, congratulating him for the role he played in this coup, I remember thinking, *if only Adam was still alive, what an influential team he and Dan would have made.*

It was also in that moment I committed to becoming a copper.

As the initial excitement waned and a fourth cuppa was being served, I noticed that Don and Fay were staring at me. The look on Fay's face intrigued me, for when she knew I held her gaze, she tilted her head slightly to one side, smiled and silently mouthed the words 'well, go on.'

'OK, OK,' I said eagerly, then somewhat impatiently added, 'so, where do I sign up Don?'

'If you wish; right here and now son,' Don replied as he retrieved a small bundle of papers from an inside pocket of his jacket. If we're lucky you might be able to greet Dan at the station as fellow police officers.'

I signed those papers immediately without the need for a second thought. However, while in the process of returning them to Don, I was suddenly set upon by Fay, Rocky, Kay, Don and Brenda, and would you believe it, by Anna and Frank Portesi who, as I learnt later, had been previously "worded up" by Don about what was about to transpire.

Initially, Charlotte sat quietly; no doubt bemused by all the attention being lavished upon her dad. Nevertheless, as soon as an opening in that crush appeared, she waddled up to me and demanded I pick her up. She suddenly kissed me on the lips, then threw her arms around my neck and damn nearly choked me, emulating what she had seen her mother do.

Though the Portesi's soon took their leave, a third bottle of Durif had somehow found its way onto the veranda table. Its contents soon evaporated.

As the afternoon likewise diminished, Don took me aside. 'That was a gutsy call you and Fay made. And you both must know that Brenda and I are personally grateful ... and ditto on behalf of our entire policing district.

'By the way, I've done some routine checks on Kay's history. Rocky'd certainly blow a gasket if he knew I did that. Just as he would if he knew I've also had a yarn with Kay, unbeknown to Rocky.

'But there's nothing to worry about I can assure you. Kay served a distinguished career with the New South Wales Police Force and operated, mostly alone, in the arrest of many felons, and was particularly active in tracking down and apprehending stock thieves. She's also sent four not so savoury standover merchants to their early graves.

'Leon, I'd like this to be kept to yourself, though I'll personally inform Dan of this conversation.

'And Kay has agreed should you need moral or physical support with your duties, then you're at liberty to seek her support ... but never so that Rocky will know what's going on. Also, be aware, as a volunteer, she has the right to refuse any request you might make; after all, she has devoted herself to Rocky.'

'Which reminds me. Sometime during the next two weeks, you'll be formally inducted into the Victorian Police Force, accompanied by a low-key ceremony to be held at The Beechworth High Security Prison.

'It won't be all beer and skittles. You'll be undergoing quite an extensive training program, but you'll manage, just as you will regarding the proper use, treatment and care of police horses ... and how to use and maintain the handgun you'll be issued, and most importantly, when to use it. Don't worry, you'll be getting plenty of practise.

'They'll also teach you some handy self-defence techniques, how to use a camera for collecting crime scene evidence ... and, with a bit of luck they'll teach you how to drive an automobile.

'Take enough changes of clothes for at least eight days. With luck, while you're there, you'll be issued with two sets of Police uniforms; one for Summer, and one for Winter.

'The contract you've signed states the pay you'll receive and eligible reimbursements. It's not great but goes up with experience and uninterrupted years of service.'

'I'm sure Fay and I will cope financially; we're not paupers.

'But hang on Don, you said there were two bits of news; pray, do tell.'

'Oh yeah. If you do receive your uniforms during that time, why not put one on and pay Mickey a visit; he's an inmate there, and you in uniform is bound to really piss him off!

'Leon, there's something else I've discussed with Rocky which you need to know about.'

'And what might that be?'

'Well, he acknowledges what's happening to him physically and mentally, but he has a genuine fear. His greatest concern, still, is what would happen to the property, and to Fay and your kids of course, should you get killed in the line of duty; and who'd take over?'

'Fay and Kay and I've already talked together about this. But look, Don, what else can I do but keep my wits about me ... and always have one up the spout?

'There'll be plenty of good options Don, but for now I'm focussed on helping Dan.'

* * *

From afar, probably twoscore yards away, I gazed upon a gang of prisoners in their formal striped working-gang clothes; their task ... breaking rocks into smaller rocks.

At one stage, Mickey stopped working, wiped the sweat from his forehead with the sleeve of his shirt and then looked about, perhaps initially, at nothing in particular.

Yet somehow his eyes suddenly became fixated upon me, resplendent in my new uniform. Mickey spat, tossed back his head in disdain I suspect, then quickly delivered a two-handed, obscene gesture directly at me.

My response? I theatrically mouthed the words, 'A rope awaits you Mickey,' while simultaneously enacting the movement a hangman might use when pulling tight the slip knot of his noose.

49

I completed the promised police training during the following couple of weeks, and I have to say, apart from the goddam paperwork requirements, I thoroughly enjoyed myself and met two blokes my own age with whom I shared common interests and with who it made sense to cultivate a close working relationship.

On the day I departed The Beechworth High Security Prison as a fully-fledged police officer, coincidently, I arrived at the same time Dan and his family arrived in Wangaratta.

However, for some time previously there had been only one paramount problem in my mind: where on earth were they going to live!?

I need not have worried, for Rocky's memory hadn't abandoned him entirely. And, as good luck sometimes lands at your feet, so too had Rocky previously learnt one of his lifelong friends, a pioneer of the Wangaratta region, had decided to retire and abruptly departed with his wife to Melbourne to see out his final days.

I never did learn what reciprocal payment arrangement must have been forged between those two men, but there was a slight sniff of some long-ago liaison with a vicar's wife, which had led to Rocky's friend being hounded out of town.

Anyway, any dispute over ownership of that vacated property was short lived when Rocky (miraculously) produced the Title of Ownership and handed it to Dan.

'Here, this's yours now son. Yah might have a bit of cleaning up to do, but basically everything should be sound and there're five bedrooms. And you've got five fully fenced acres for yah horses, plus there's stables and all the shedding you'll need.'

'Bloody hell Rocky, I wasn't expecting this,' said Dan sheepishly, 'but thank you, most generous of you.'

Having introduced his family all round, it quickly became obvious everyone was on for a chat. However, Rocky suddenly called out, 'Come on folks, let's get this tired mob moving. There's going to be plenty of time to talk later. Follow us, Dan; your place is only a mile out of town and by the look of things you'll need a hand to unload.'

But that wasn't Rocky's only surprise.

As we approached the property, a shiny new motor vehicle could be seen parked beside the house: a Ford sedan.

Genuinely surprised, I called out to Dan as we dismounted. 'Your first visitors already mate?'

'Be buggered!' Rocky replied with a broad and happy expression on his weathered face. 'Here, Dan, I understand you'll need these.'

Dan, flabbergasted I reckon, hesitantly accepted the two keys Rocky handed to him.

'Use it wisely son,' Rocky said meaningfully, then busied himself releasing some of the ropes which secured Dan's many possessions to his horse.

Much later that afternoon, we'd done all we could to get Dan and his family settled, and now the five of us were on the way back to our property, tired and hoping we'd arrive home before it got dark.

'You do realise, my darling wife, that there's still a few problems to resolve?' I said quietly to Fay, who was now leaning against me while cuddling our very sleepy daughter.

'Like what?'

'Well, and this is a biggy. There's no way I want to be trooping into and out of Wang every day to go to work, and I don't want to be on my own during the week living in a boarding house, no matter how nice it might be.'

'Yeah, fair enough, but I'm too tired to discuss that right now. When we get home, I'll put Charlotte to bed, then I'll put the kettle on for a cuppa; we can talk about it then.'

I eventually got to sleep that night, albeit long after Fay had handed me a set of keys for the brand new, white de Soto utility parked outside our cottage. Fay and Rocky had obviously been in cahoots: talk about a day of surprises!

I know I've said it before, but I recall thinking ... *what on God's earth had I done to deserve such generosity.*

50

Don made little fuss about his retirement. Rather, he took a hands-off approach and left the day-to-day running of the police station, attending to local grievances, putting an end to alcohol inflamed fights and handling written communications to Dan and me.

What I did not expect was Don's insistence that we accompany him on street walks and visits to outlying farms to introduce us, and to seek the cooperation of people in keeping our district safe and free of conflict.

His presence at the station though minimal and gradually reducing, did not deny us access to him any day, at any time, if we seriously needed his advice.

What impressed me was Dan's authoritative patience and his ability to discuss matters in clear and concise English. His stature may not have intimidated many, but his commitment, in general, impressed most.

I had my own way of dealing fairly and occasionally forcibly with people, but never in a stand-overish manner, though mind you, by this time I possessed a sizable, well-muscled physique.

Our principal objective in most situations was to have everyone recognise that Dan and I represented a formidable team operating on behalf of the public and that it was not in their best interests to clam up. Generally, we could get most people talking as long as they had confidence in us that anything we were told, would remain private.

* * *

THERE WAS one interesting occurrence which Dan and I took many weeks to put to rest. Leads and possible sightings of eighteen stolen cattle took us out of the stifling heat of the Wangaratta Police Station and into the vast, much cooler climate of the Barry Ranges regions and areas of the Hotham High Plains with which Dan and I were familiar.

In keeping with a tradition initiated by the Beverage brothers who lived in, and leased thousands of acres of the Buckland Valley and surrounding alpine grazing country, they would round up eighteen wild bulls and truck them in two trucks to the Myrtleford show-ground, to be used in the New Years Day rodeo. Having off-loaded their bulls, the Beverage brothers would then drive their empty trucks back to their farmhouse in the Buckland Valley.

The rodeo not only attracted people from all over Victoria, but Australia wide. Beverage bulls had, over the preceding years, earned a fearsome reputation for their huge size, strength and crazed hatred of mankind, which in turn attracted the best professional bull riders, thinking they could earn a quick quid or two.

At the conclusion of this year's rodeo, the bulls were scheduled to be returned to the Beverage property via appointed contractors who would release the bulls back into the wilds of the Beverage leasehold.

But that failed to eventuate.

Reliable witnesses had seen the bulls being loaded at the Myrtle-ford show ground, but did not recognise the men involved; nor whose trucks were being used, just the name of the truck manufacturer.

The only substantial lead we could agree upon was that the trucks had to have been switched. When questioned, the Beverage brothers swore blind they had no idea where their stock was. It was a convincing display, until the younger brother unwittingly gave us the information we needed. 'How would we know where our cattle have disappeared to; they could be anywhere, in Warrnambool for all we know!?'

Dan winked at me, then politely asked the brothers what their plans were for the next weekend so that we could sit around a table and have a good yarn about what happened to their bulls.

Whilst both agreed to that meeting, both were "no shows".

* * *

IT WAS several months later when Don arrived one afternoon to relay some unrelated but otherwise interesting news to us.

'I've just learned Mickey's still currently being held at the maximum-security prison in Beechworth,' Dan announced, but quickly added, 'and his multiple charges will all be heard in Melbourne before separate judges and juries.

'Those trials have been scheduled for about twelve months down the track, but the word around the traps is that Mickey will be found guilty on all charges and sentenced to be hung. Not unexpected, eh?

'Regardless, he won't be giving grief to anyone for a long time.'

* * *

IT WAS during those early days as a police officer, that Fay, Kay, Dan's wife Leah and I, all struck up strong and lasting friendships, as it would so become the case with their kids Archie and Zoe, and Charlotte, and with our son when he eventually decided to grace us with his company.

Leah and Fay, as-near-as-damn-it the same age, quickly learnt how to drive motor vehicles; fast and daring and with great skill I was assured.

On occasions when Dan and I were away on horseback patrols, they volunteered to drive to remote properties where in the first instance a farmer who had been crushed by an angry bull needed to be driven to the Albury hospital for urgent medical treatment. The second case involved a very pregnant woman who needed immediate support and who was then driven at breakneck speed to the Wangaratta bush nursing hospital where it was known a midwife was on call.

Max and Elspeth were struggling with their increasing infirmities, but they were also neighbours no more than a mile from Dan and Leah's house. So, whenever Fay visited Leah, together they'd call on Fay's parents ... usually with Charlotte in tow.

51

With the passage of time, work routines at the police station, followed by weekend farm duties, evolved in lock step with socialising with our faithful neighbours. Life was good.

The most anticipated, memorable and proud event occurred when our second beautiful child arrived: on time and the right gender, exactly as Anna Portesi had forecast.

Initially, Adam was more boisterous than Charlotte had been, but no less inquisitive as the weeks and months rolled on. It was interesting how Adam, when only a few months old was always elated to be around horses. Our ever-trustworthy Walers would, for example, sniff Adam's hands or his head, then for no apparent reason, whinny softly and nod their heads ... as if giving approval of this tiny boy.

* * *

NEVERTHELESS, tragedy struck three times within eight months of young Adam's arrival.

Regrettably, Elspeth and Max, Fay's parents and my stepparents, both passed away, as did Rocky.

People argue that time cures all; perhaps it does, but as much as you think you are prepared to handle the passing of such wonderful human beings, it does nothing to comfort you when suddenly confronted with the *actual* event.

In Elspeth's and Max's case, they died about three weeks apart. Both had suddenly lost significant weight which did nothing to relieve their physical discomfort. Both were essentially bed-ridden, could not walk even short distances without assistance because they had lost almost all sense of balance and worse, both were almost blind. Though neither complained, their biggest upset was being reliant upon others to feed them, wash them and attend to cleaning up after their uncontrollable and embarrassing toilet accidents.

Actually, Max died about two weeks after Elspeth. While holding my hand he said with considerable difficulty, 'You've been a wonderful son, Leon. Please, look after Fay and your kids.' His eye lids then fluttered, and he was gone.

But that's not how I wanted to remember them for they had been my providers, protectors and confidants, as if they had been my birth parents.

Fay too was philosophical about their passing; her biggest ordeal was remaining calm when Charlotte's curiosity surfaced wanting to know where her nanna and poppa were hiding.

Elspeth and Max were buried in the same grave site.

* * *

HOWEVER, my greatest loss was Rocky.

It was unsettling to watch his illness dominate his life: it hit hard and fast.

Yet, before that affliction overcame him completely, he still had some golden moments of comprehension. I was so glad to be with him frequently enough not to have missed something bordering on incredible which I can neither explain, nor will I ever forget.

It was late summer and mid-afternoon on a typical Northeast Victorian day; still shorts and sleeveless shirt weather. A gentle breeze rustled the leaves in the canopy of the two huge eucalypts which cast their shadows over the homestead roof. Rocky called out to me. 'I say, son, givus yah arm. I'd like ta go 'an sit by our creek for a while.'

At a bend which enabled us to watch trout rise through the crystal-clear water to take an unsuspecting grasshopper or nymph, we'd sit comfortably side by side on the creek bank. This place had become our favourite place above any other, where we said nothing, or shared the occasional confidence.

'Yah do realise Leon, that it's two years ago ta day that Adam left us?'

'Yep, I do actually. And do you remember this is exactly where Adam first taught me how to catch trout, using grasshoppers or mud-eyes for bait?'

Rocky's reply was an almost inaudible, yet contented, 'ehhmm.'

Another half hour expired without further conversation. But then, just as I was considering asking Rocky whether he might now like to return to the homestead, for no particular reason I looked up at the clouds gathering way overhead.

There, soaring just within view was a lone wedge tailed eagle. 'Hey Rocky,' I asked while casually pointing to where I had last seen the eagle. 'Look, there's *Bunjil*, can you see him?'

Rocky never replied, but as I lowered my gaze, there, about forty yards upstream Adam and a dingo appeared, standing side by side; not ghost like, but nearly as clear as in real life.

Adam was dressed in his mob's traditional animal skin clothing and holding a large boomerang.

I glanced at Rocky. There was no doubt in my mind he was looking exactly where I was. About five or so seconds later Adam smiled broadly, raised the boomerang above his head, then waded across the creek, his spectre and that of the dingo fading as they disappeared into the surrounding scrub.

I felt neither fear nor threatened at what I had just witnessed. I gently nudged Rocky with the intention of asking him if he too had seen those images, but he simply replied, 'Do I know that fella?'

Without thinking why, I again glanced up at the sky, just in time to see *Bunjil* drifting away on the warm afternoon breeze.

* * *

ROCKY PASSED AWAY THAT NIGHT, but how did I know that?

Well, the following morning, I rose early intending to relieve myself. However, as I walked from the house I damn nearly walked into Jimmie, frightening the hell out of me.

'Leon my brother, it not time to be afraid. My mob we have Rocky. He now together with Adam resting in safe place you know about. He was good man, like you, maybe tonight we sing to him in his Dreamtime.

52

Though I'd held some thoughts of one day moving to New South Wales; to perhaps Dorrigo, Newcastle or even further north to the sunshine coastline of southern Queensland, I no longer yearned to be living somewhere else. It was now obvious to me that I'd been dreaming the wrong dream: everyone I loved and everything I owned and had worked hard to secure were right under my nose.

Family life settled into a pattern no doubt the envy of others; but never that of our amazing friends, Anna and Frank Portesi, and Dan and Leah Cameron. What an incredible, disparate mix of people; English, colonial Australian, Italian and indigenous aboriginal folk ... all the greatest of friends who preferred to be called, Australian.

I was grateful that my chosen career as a police officer exempted me from serving as a soldier in the First World War, and it infuriated me when I met several former farmers who had returned home from that conflict either badly maimed or mentally overwhelmed from their experiences. None deserved the unrecognized penalty of living out their lives in those incurable bodies.

I discussed this with Kay. She too was deeply saddened, and it wasn't more than a month after having met some of those men locally that she took their plight so much to heart, she announced her intention to register as a nurse in the hope her medical training, albeit minimal, might help alleviate the suffering, at least, for some.

Kay moved to Melbourne, with our blessings and understanding of course, got the nursing job she wanted at a major military rehabilitation centre and took it upon herself to supervise that centre's large quantity meals preparation.

I never again met Kay, but Fay and I exchanged correspondence with her up until we learnt of her death from natural causes after she relocated from Melbourne to Perth in Western Australia.

53

We were living busy and contented lives, but it was becoming increasingly evident our cottage was too small for our family. Since the homestead was now vacant, it made perfectly good sense that we re-inhabit it, besides Fay was pregnant again.

But about six months after that relocation, everything peaceful nearly ended.

Dan had been interviewing one of the prison guards who worked at the Beechworth prison; a likeable bloke I had met during my officer induction training there, and who I knew was looking for an opportunity to get away from prison culture: just the bloke to unburden Dan and I from the never-ending red tape of managing a police station.

Suitably impressed, Dan had offered the job to that chap, and no sooner had they shaken hands agreeing upon a potential start date, than the Prison Governor rushed up to Dan and handed him a telegram he'd just received, which, in essence said: *somehow, Mickey had escaped from custody ... only a few weeks before he was scheduled to be hung!*

* * *

WE'D LATER LEARN the details of how Mickey performed his escape, but not surprisingly in his wake he left one guard close to death and another requiring urgent dental treatment.

However, what was evident, he must have had outside assistance to have so easily eluded police efforts to locate him, let alone recapture him before he could re-offend.

Though Dan and I swept our region of responsibility on different occasions, we found nothing that might indicate he was lurking in our area, and not a single sighting of him was reported to us.

Others were more successful.

An unidentified, middle-aged woman found dead six months later, near Mansfield, may have been Mickey's accomplice; her murder, a bullet in the back of her head was obviously not suicide and had all the hallmarks of Mickey's manic disrespect for human life.

While on a routine patrol, Police officers from Packenham, a small settlement much closer to Melbourne, searched an abandoned shack and found evidence confirming that place to have been the residence of the murdered woman ... and evidence she'd been co-existing with an unidentified male.

The nearest neighbours, albeit half a mile away, were aware of that circumstance, but had never met that bloke, though verbal descriptions of Mickey's appearance provided by me seemed to gel with their recollections.

Following the discovery of that woman's murder, no further information was received by the police which might have led to Mickey's capture.

In fact, Mickey remained at bay for another six or seven months, and although the threat of him returning to seek revenge upon me and my family was ever possible, that eventuality did not dominate our lives.

54

Spring had sprung and Fay and I (and our ever-attentive supervisors, Charlotte and Adam) were working in our home garden planting, weeding and liberally pouring my secret fertiliser everywhere (a liquid blend of horse and cattle shit) to give "the new stuff" a good start to the season, when Anna and Frank Portesi arrived in their buggy.

'Comma on you two kids,' Frank called, 'or you'll missa da party. Quick a like, jump ona board.'

Charlotte and Adam grabbed the neatly wrapped presents Fay had prepared for the oldest Portesi boy and they joyously wasted no time scrambling onto the buggy.

'We'll come over and collect 'em about four o'clock. Is that OK, Anna?' Fay called.'

'Yeah. That a be perfek, see you then. Frank, this a ugly brute, he a rekon there just might be another bottle to inspect.'

Frank winked, smiled mischievously in my direction then urged his horse into a decent trot amid much waving and happy shouts of *see yah* from the party goers.

By this time, Fay was leaning against me with one arm firmly around my back. I reciprocated and glanced at her. Tears were running down her cheeks; mine soon followed but nothing else was said until the horse and buggy was out of sight.

'I love you heaps, Leon.'

'But not as much as I love you, Fay. I'm a very lucky man.'

* * *

WE TOOK an early lunch break after which Fay decided to rest her eyes. I returned to the garden to finish watering in our plantings.

But before getting too involved, I couldn't resist watching the graceful manoeuvres of a pair of wedgetail eagles high above; circling, gliding and probably thoroughly enjoying themselves.

Not long after, I heard the unmistakeable sound of an approaching horse and buggy. *'Surely,'* I thought, *'that can't be the Portesi's; they've only just left.*

It wasn't the Portesi's.

But it *was* a buggy, a grand one at that. And just one bloke on board, dressed very much the dandy with polished boots, spats, well-tailored clothes, a hideous straw hat and sporting a shiny walking stick.

'Nearly got pushed from the road back there,' he said as he dismounted then briskly twirled his walking stick, I think to big note himself. 'Four in a buggy that small and going so insanely fast can be a tad dangerous, you should know that.'

'That'll be our kids going to a birthday party at our neighbour's place. So, what can I do for you? I asked, ignoring his overbearing attitude.

'Oh, come on Leon, you must recognise me, surely?'

'Well, no I don't; should I?'

'I'm your goddam brother, Bertie!'

'Is that right? I don't recall inviting you here.'

'Don't be like that Leon. I didn't come here to see you; I came to see my parents.'

'Ah, yes. Now the penny drops. Come to think of it you could be Bertie, not that I care two hoots.

'Mind you, if you say you're my stepbrother, I broke that tie many, many years ago. And you're too late to see your parents, they both died some time ago. You broke their hearts, but I suppose that means nought to you.

'And should it be an inheritance you're after, there was none ... so you may as well get back in your buggy and piss off.'

'Now you're being entirely obtuse Leon, I'm in no need of an inheritance, nor do I appreciate your attitude, Leon.

'Then perhaps I should do what Rocky suggested and knock your rotten block off.'

We were about to square off, when I heard Fay yell from inside the house, 'Leon, can you smell smoke?'

That's when I should have punched Bertie on his nose, for he dropped his guard, stared towards the house and said, genuinely surprised, 'My god, is that Fay?'

'Bertie!?' Fay asked quizzically as she stepped from the front veranda.

'Unfortunately, it is. Ignore him Fay, he's just leaving.'

Totally ignoring me, Bertie walked towards Fay. As he was about to hug his sister, she vigorously thrust both of her hands onto his chest, sending him staggering backwards.

'Like I said, Bertie, you're not welcome here; and you're a damn slow learner. Get on your buggy and leave this minute or I'll kick your arse all the way to the front gate.'

'Hang on a second, darling', Fay said, alarmed. 'Look, behind you! That's smoke and it looks like it's bloody well coming from our cottage.'

55

Somehow the three of us made it onto the buggy. Bertie thrashed the reins over the horse's back and it leapt forward, only to be aggressively turned in the direction of the fire and receive another whack.

It was our cabin burning, and already in an unrecoverable stage of destruction. Huge flames, and trails of sparks were sharing the space above the cottage with an enormous cloud of black, white and brown smoke. The noise of the fire was horrific, and the heat generated made it impossible to approach, let alone attempt to save anything from the cottage ... even if we had a complete fire brigade on hand.

As the cottage collapsed sending a massive upheaval of sparks racing skyward, a sarcastic voice behind us penetrated the spectacle before us.

'What a bloody shame, I bet that was such a cosy little shack. But it ain't no more, eh'.

I knew that voice. Mickey! Geezus! Now what?!

We three spun in unison to confront that devil, but there was nothing we could do; he was armed with a multi-round rifle ... whereas we had nothing to defend ourselves, so it seemed.

'None of yah's leavin' 'ere, so who's goin' first. What about you Leon, yah useless bastard, thinking that wearing a copper's uniform makes yah hero material ... which yah ain't. And not only are you a lousy black fella lover to boot, but I'm Rocky's son, not you! This place should be mine.

'Or what about you, pretty boy; all dressed up like fried bread. Geeze, I'd like ta go a few rounds with you; I'd teach yah what's right, yah poofter!

'And here's that blond slut; I've often wondered how you'd go under my pump.'

Fay spat at Mickey; I'd never seen her do that before!

Mickey laughed hideously, put one up the spout, then cocked and levelled his rifle directly at me.

In the few seconds remaining before I met my maker, I didn't pray, but I looked at Fay's beautiful face; tears were now being forced between her closed eyelids.

Most unexpectedly, I suddenly heard the high-pitched screech of a wedge tailed eagle. I opened my eyes just in time to see *Bunjil* latch his huge, sharp talons onto Mickey's right forearm.

In between the furious beating of *Bunjil's* huge wings around Mickey's face, and his subsequent tortured screaming, his rifle discharged, thankfully missing my head by no more than the thickness of a cigarette paper.

In what seemed a well-rehearsed movement, Bertie grabbed the body of his walking stick in one hand, and then, while twisting the knob of the stick with the other hand, he withdrew a long, slender blade of glistening steel.

With Mickey clearly distracted, without further ado Bertie lunged forward and thrust that blade into Mickey's chest; so hard in fact that it protruded at least ten inches from his back ... a performance reminiscent of a bullfighting matador committing to the *coup de grâce*.

The look on Mickey's face was priceless; a blend of shock, anguish and of desperately trying to recall something unspoken. Good riddance to bad rubbish, I say!

Where credit's due, Bertie had bravely redeemed himself;

returning to my short list of people whom I greatly respected and who would forever be a friend.

I checked Mickey's clothing and found sufficient documents to identify him. There was also a death notice newspaper clipping about Elspeth's and Max's passing in a back pocket, which I concluded in my best investigative manner, was all the information Mickey needed to locate and kill me.

A strong, drawn-out screech suddenly filled the air.

Looking up, there was *Bunjil* soaring overhead, albeit now heading towards Mount Buffalo.

I waved in appreciation, not expecting he would tilt his wings from side to side in acknowledgement, but goddamn it, he did.

Turning to Bertie I then said, 'So, why exactly did you decide to pay us a visit?'

THE END

AUTHOR'S NOTE

The protagonist in this novel, Mickey, was a potential contender for inclusion in my fifth novel, "God Only knows When" which casts an eye over the criminal underbelly of rural Australia.

However, out of respect for the Farm Invasion and Livestock Theft Inspectors of the Victorian Police Force and given that Mickey's notoriety has never been reported in the public domain, his omission from that novel was obviously necessary.

I make no assertions of fact, that this novel solves the truth surrounding multiple murders at the remote Wonnangatta Station in NE Victoria, sometime between late 1917, and the end of 1918.

However, it does suggest a high degree of probability which perhaps opens alternative lines of investigation to pursue for both the Victorian and New South Wales Police forces

Should you wish to read my other novels, they are all available to purchase in print book and eBook formats, direct from my website:
www.trevortuckerpublishing.com.au

ACKNOWLEDGMENTS

Tony Park. Entrepreneur and internationally acclaimed author of 22 amazing novels, plus 5 "factual accounts" written together with some seriously interesting and devoted people. Thanks, mate, for giving me the opportunity to ensure my sixth novel will see the light of day.

Jamie Robinson. JAR digital. My right-hand man who developed my new, fantastic interactive website. Thanks also Jamie for freely applying your commercial skills.

Melissa Bridges. *hello@yes lets write.* My left-hand lady. Without you Mellissa, I would not have ventured into social media. So, thanks heaps for your support, your steadying influence and for walking me through what's needed to build a successful Facebook page.

Leandra Wicks. Cover designer. I greatly appreciate your extraordinary, eye-catching and beautiful artwork. Thanks so much.

Thomas Crosby. iT guru. Without your patience, teachings and software management skills, this novel and my previous 2 books would probably have been abandoned.

Callum Tucker. My son, the critique. Thanks again Call, for allowing me to bounce aspects of this novel off you. Also, it really is appreciated that everything you suggested was **not** 'really good dad.'

ABOUT THE AUTHOR

Inspired by the joy and intense satisfaction of writing my first five novels, "*Ned Kelly's Son*", "*The Stolen maps... Australia's greatest maritime secret?*", "*Aussie Anecdotes*", "*A Sense of Justice*" and "*God Only Knows When*"—plus the success of their sales—I embarked upon my sixth authorial adventure.

Wonnangatta came about through conflicting anecdotal comments, incomplete research notes and that no evidence has ever been agreed as proof positive who perpetrated two unsolved murders of men who worked together at the remote Wonnangatta Station in Northeast Victoria. Clearly, they could not have murdered each other, so another party or party's must have been involved. Who, and exactly how many people were murdered in the high country during the period which ran in parallel with the First World War, remains unknown.

For me, writing is a most satisfying outlet for creativity ... both challenging, and relaxing. However, writing is not escapism, but rather the compulsion of a glorious illness which I call, **The Dreamer's Disease,** i.e., that the more you create, the more you receive.

Having retired from the oil and gas industry, my other interests include when possible, spending time with my kids, and grandkids, fishing, reading, bike riding, watching Test cricket and AFL football (in both men's and women's formats), and listening to classical music ... but most of all, enjoying the life-changing experiences of travelling the world.

If you enjoyed Wonnangatta, take a look at Trevor's other books on the following pages.

Ned Kelly's Son
By Trevor Tucker

Beautiful, headstrong Orla O'Meara escapes persecution in 19th century Ireland to start a new life in the wild colony of Victoria, Australia.

There she meets the continent's most notorious bushranger, Ned Kelly and a brief, passionate relationship results in the birth of the outlaw's unknown son, Niall.

After Ned's violent death, Orla and her son have to learn to survive in this tough, unforgiving land. Their travels, together with a faithful Waler horse named Boss Boy, take them throughout Australia and bring them up against criminals, goldminers, loggers and the police.

Ned Kelly's Son is a sweeping saga, following mother and son and the family's descendants through Australia's transition from a collection of colonies to a nation born during the Boer War, in which Niall serves.

The Kellys fight injustice and champion the rights of aboriginal people through a hundred years of struggle, poverty, romance, wealth, pain and redemption.

The Stolen Maps
By Trevor Tucker

It is 1519 and two intrepid Portuguese seafarers set off on separate missions to different parts of the globe. Their journeys intersect with the European discovery of 'The Great South Land'.

Manny Perez, young and adventurous, and Cristo de Mendonça an older, experienced naval officer, become friends and agree to map the east coast of this wild continent, unknown to white people.

Danger and death await on land and sea as the explorers make contact with the indigenous people of this strange new place, and face the worst that nature can hurl at their ships.

Lost, re-drawn, then stolen, Manny and Cristo's precious maps become a treasure sought after in a race between empires.

Heroism, tragedy, romance and intrigue reverberate all the way through history, leading to the discovery of a secret lying buried beneath modern Australia's coastal sands.

A Sense of Justice
By Trevor Tucker

Two young Englishmen, Harry Taylor, a minor felon, and Patrick Galbraith, a navy marine lieutenant serving on the final convict transport ship bound for Australia in 1867, become friends on the voyage.

Harry and Patrick both end up in Trial Bay Prison on the north coast of New South Wales.

In return for good behaviour, an early release allows them to explore the hinterland. Opportunity knocks when the pair have a violent run-in with bushrangers and land a windfall beyond their wildest dreams.

But their newfound wealth also haunts their adventurous lives, through a series of pivotal encounters with cattle thieves, murderers, colourful figures of the colony's racing and farming industries, and a young Aboriginal woman.

Harry and Patrick both find love in the arms of beautiful women, but their good fortune comes under threat when a ghost from their past emerges.

God Only Knows When
By Trevor Tucker

Failed farmer Andy Stevens' life takes a turn for the better when he meets and marries Sydney barrister Beth Carmichael, but before they can settle into their new life the couple is recruited by the Federal Government as Livestock Theft Investigation officers.

Livestock theft – sheep and cattle rustling – is the thriving but little-known sinister underbelly of Australian rural life.

Along with their leader, Beau, a no-nonsense former drover, two high-flying young army officers and an aboriginal investigator, the team tackle stock theft head-on and commence a hunt for a killer who is preying on Australian farmers and taking their land.

The criminal web they uncover is far reaching and diverse, encompassing native bird and reptile smuggling, counterfeiting and even a fine-art racket dating back to the Second World War.

Even as their successes mount, Andy, Beth and their teammates have to watch their backs. Who knows who is really pulling the strings?

Reader review: "A thoroughly enjoyable read. Trevor has embraced a significant topic which is often overlooked and seldom, if ever, understood by those who do not live in regional Australia."